Life

Beyond

Circumstance

By

Jullian Smallwood

All Rights Reserved

copyright©2019

By Jullian Smallwood

No part of this Book may be reproduced, stored in a retrieval system, or transmitted by any means, electronic, mechanical, photocopying, recording, or otherwise, without written permission from the author.

ISBN: softcover   978-1-6492-1344-0

Table of content

Chapter 1.... Troublesome

Chapter 2... Steps

Chapter 3... Humanity

Chapter 4... Acts of Kindness.

Chapter 5... Natives & Invaders

Chapter 6... Heartaches

Chapter 7... Psychological warfare

Chapter 8... The nephew

Chapter 9... The Africans

Chapter 10... The New Chief

Chapter 11... Freedom Run.

Chapter 12... Vengeful

Chapter 13... Landscape

Chapter 14... A Dying Request

Chapter 15... Town on Fire

Table of content

Chapter 16... Revenge

Chapter 17... Harlem

Chapter 18... Maturity

Chapter 19... Evolvement

Chapter 20... Prepared

Chapter 21... Accolades

Chapter 22... Chief

Chapter 23... Inheritance

Chapter 24... Humanitarians

Chapter 25... Building

Chapter 26... Pay Back.

Chapter 27... Pork Chop

Chapter 28... Father's side

Chapter 29... Woman Chief

Chapter 30... Identity

This book is dedicated to the unknown, forgotten people of the world. Also, to the people who lost their identity due to many different circumstances. To the people who lost their history and culture. Last, but not least, this book is dedicated to you. The reader…

Jullian Smallwood

Chapter 1
Troublesome

As Mike could recall, his mother **and** father were in an abusive and drug infested relationship. Growing up with both parents being addicted to drugs was difficult to begin with. His father always called his mother his beautiful Indian queen. Him and his siblings never understood what he meant by that.

Mainly, because most of the time, when he said that, he was high. So, they assumed it was just high talk. Where they lived at, was a rough neighborhood, crime and drugs were everywhere.

The apartment building, they lived in looked like an old ran down, abandoned building. Ran down was a good way of saying it, because it was beyond that. The landlord did not care. Mainly, he did not want to be bothered.

Mike and his brother had to come to the realization, their parents were what people called, crackheads. They did not like it, but it was their reality.

And just like that, one day their father just upped and left them. His mother had to deal with the 4 children she had with their father. But also, her own demons.

She kept it together more than anyone, would have ever given her credit for. Even due to the fact, that her baby father left her.

Her drug abuse turned for the worst. Many days, Mike and his older brother would walk home from school. On their way home they would see their mother get into different men cars.

They picked up their younger sisters from the babysitter. They would eat cereal for dinner. Most of the time, their mother came home late at night too high to do anything.

As the boys grew well into their teenage years. Mike's brother wanted to protect their mother as much as possible. He did not like the fact that, their mother was selling her body for drugs.

Eventually his brother hooked up with a well-known drug dealer, who used to deal, and date, their mom, every now and again. Mike's brother began to sell drugs for this individual.

He explained to Mike, that was the only way he knew how to protect their mother and create money to run the household. By selling drugs and support their mother's drug habit.

He felt like it was the best thing to do. He told his little brother, at least they did not have to worry about their mother doing, God knows what, to get high.

Their mother had a part-time job at the local discount store. Whenever she was able to function. Sometimes she would steal necessities for the household. The manager would let her do whatever she wanted if he did whatever he wanted sexually.

Mike's brother learned a lot about the drug game for the man he was working for. So, when the drug dealer his brother was working for, got murdered, he had already learned and knew how to sell drugs for himself.

He knew the connection, the person to purchase the drugs from. With knowing the ends and outs of the drug game. Eventually, his brother opened a crack spot in the building they lived at.

They went from not having nothing, to at least having food on the table, and food in the refrigerator. His brother made money, but nothing big. Basically, he made just enough to make ends meet. And to keep their mother off the streets.

As things was about to be okay, it always seems to turn worst. His brother got arrested for selling drugs. His brother was sentenced to 10 years in prison. Due to the fact his brother got caught selling drugs in the building they lived in, Mike's mother lost their apartment in the building, in the process.

One thing that Mike's brother always taught him, was not to do what he did. With not too much was coming in, it became a dark time in Mike's life. Mike's graduation quickly approached. He did not have anything to wear to his high school graduation ceremony.

Thank God for his grandmother. She provided her grandson with a pair of dress pants, a dress shirt and pair of dress shoes. She did not want him to miss out on one of the most important days of his young life.

A letter came to the apartment. Mike had won an all-paid scholarship to college. He won the scholarship by writing an essay about what he wanted to do in his life and how he wanted to help others.

He wrote about becoming an author. He explains, he wanted more people to read, the ones who mostly do not read. Also, he wanted to write books with true meanings to them. His thoughts where reading is fundamental.

Especially, in the inner urban cities through-out America, illiteracy was at an alarming rate. He was a little nervous when he had to read his essay in front of an audience at the scholarship award show.

Even though he wore the same outfit at both events. But that was not important at the time. What was important, was he had won a full scholarship to attend a local community college, in the borough, he was a resident of, in New York City.

His mother stood there with tears in her eyes. The day turned out to be a great day. The joy and happiness over what Mike did was short lived.

They moved into a city shelter a few days later. A couple of weeks later, his mother got caught buying some drugs.

The only reason why, the city did not come to the shelter, and place Mike and his sisters into child protection services. Was because, Mike was 18 at the time. With no one else to turn to, Mike called his grandmother for help.

His grandmother bailed his mother out, the next day after she saw the judge. To Mike and his sisters, they felt like the shelter was better than where they were living before.

His grandmother went to court with his mother. His mother took a plea deal, she was placed on a year probation and was ordered to go to a day treatment program for a year. As an outpatient. She agreed to the terms of her release.

Mike's mother always looked at life, as a moving motion, like waves in an ocean. She always reminded her kids to think about life like that. She came home and sat down with her kids, she promised to do better.

She did mention, she was going through a process, that was not going to be easy. She was not going to deny that. Beyond it all, her kids knew deep down inside, they mother loved them, and she was going to try hard to get herself together. Her children just wanted their mother to get clean once and for all.

She began her day treatment that next Monday morning. This was the beginning of the summer. Everyone who knew her, who really cared about her, supported her. All pitch in to help her along the process.

Even the social worker who was assigned to her housing case push her paperwork forward towards getting an apartment. The family stood together to deal with this troublesome time.

The shelter life lasted a short time. It was short lived. So was their mother's freedom. Going to a drug rehabilitation day treatment program as an outpatient, is not always good for everyone.

At first, his mother was doing well. She started her process of detoxing the drugs out of her system.

It was going great until she had to be around other rehabbing drug addicts.

During group discussions, she met a guy, who participated in the group too. Most were recovering addicts. The two of them, hit it off very well. They began dating. The problem with that was, he really was not trying to get off drugs.

The only reason why he did the program was to stay out of jail. He began to do drugs in front of her. Eventually, she succumbed to the temptations that was presented to her. She played it off for a couple of months.

She got caught one day by one of the security officers, while entering the shelter building. when they discovered she was high, on drugs? They called the police. They came and arrested her.

Mike and his sisters had to leave the shelter. Because of their mother, they got kicked out of the shelter, and now they were homeless.

They went to live with their grandmother. In their grandmother's little one-bedroom apartment in the projects. His mother was released the following day.

A few days later, she was re-arrested by her probation officer, for failing a random drug test. This time when she saw the judge, the judge was not so lenient with her. He sentenced her to two years in prison.

Everyone was shocked to say the least. Mike and his sisters began to live with his grandmother. Mike could not help but to feel homeless.

He knew, technically he was. With all that was going on, he remembers a couple of things his mother always used to say to them, first, when there is an ending, there is always a new beginning on the way.

Also, to help people who we are less fortunate than you, even if you believe you have nothing. There is always someone who has less than you. Also, always be kind and giving to others...

Chapter 2

Steps

Mike's first day of college came, his grandmother told him, how proud of him she was. She tells him, he was not the first of the family to go to college. But she wanted him to be the first to complete college.

Even though they both knew it was a bittersweet moment. Since his mother was incarcerated. Living off his grandmother's social security check was not easy for anyone.

As far as, back to school shopping went. He told his grandmother not to worry about him. He just needed some notebooks and pens. His book bag from last year was still good. He was more concerned about his sisters.

Luckily, by the time it was time for his sisters to start school, the public assistance check came in the mail. To be honest, welfare saved the day.

Mike's major in college was journalism. He was told by his guidance counselor in high school, this is what the average writer's major was in college. So, he knew, he was making the right steps to becoming a writer, some day in the future. He knew how to write extremely well already. Writing came natural to him.

But truth be told, he did not have a clue on how to author a book. Let alone, having a story worthy enough to write. Plus, being good enough to eventually land a publishing contract. He understood, he had to take one step at a time.

His plans were to go to his college classes in the daytime. Get a job after his classes end for the day. He attended his classes for the day, then he searched for a job.

At this point at time, to be honest, a job was more important. When it came down to his current situation in life. He knew a job for him, would be an entry to the workforce. Yes, it would provide money, but it would only be like a quick fix.

But with a college degree, he could have a career. He promised himself, that one day, when he was not busy. He would go and pay his mother a visit.

His knew mother did not always make the smartest decisions. He got that, but that was his mom, he loves and cares about her. He was trying his best to place himself in a position to help his grandmother with his sisters.

He landed a job as a stock clerk at the local neighborhood supermarket. Even though his grandmother did receive food stamps for his sisters. But not for him.

Mainly, because his sisters were of age. Having a job at the supermarket with employee's discount helped a lot. No matter what, his mother always had a positive outlook on things. She felt like things will get better.

That was enough inspiration to keep them going, despite their current conditions. Which made everything a lot easier to cope with. Which led to less pressure on the brain, less things to worry about.

With that notion it can go a long way. After he receives his second paycheck, he decided to go upstate to visit his mother in prison. Seeing his mother being brought out to the visiting room with chains and shackles on her feet.

It was surreal to him. he could not understand why? She was not a harden criminal. First, he had to get this off his chest. He tells her, she left him and his little sisters homeless, because she thought selfishly.

She sat and listened. Then she lets him know, where they all were at, now, was not no way in the world, their destination.

She states this looking right into her son's eyes. Even where she was at, she tells him, none of this defines them, as humans. However, not smart choices will get you in places like this.

She asks about everyone, including her mother. He told her about the start of his college career and his job, he got. She was pleased to hear all of what he had to say. He mentions his sister was getting taller and bigger by the days.

His mother was hurt, of the fact, of not being there to see her little girls growing up. The realization of recklessness on her behalf got her in the predicament she was in. She had no one to blame but herself. It was a hard pill to swallow.

Prison was her reality, she had to deal with for the moment. Before he left, he informed her that he was placing some money in her prison commissary. She smiled, she wanted him to know, she loves him. She also thanked him for the money he was giving.

The visit made her feel good and low. It was necessary for this to happen. The day was okay for Mike. He accomplishes what he set out to do. That was enough for him.

For Mike some days, his schedule was tight with school and work. Especially, when he had a lot of classes during the day. Luckily for him, it only took place a couple times in a week.

He held the notion that with hard work, dedication, sacrifice, blood, sweat, and tears was expendable when it came down to the bigger picture. And that was Mike's goals, he wanted to achieve.

Chapter 3
Humanity

Mike's average mornings began with him placing his little sisters on their school bus. Then he walks to the train station to catch the train to school. He swipes his metro card, turns the turnstile, as he proceeds to walk through. He walks down the stairs to the platform. He looks, into the train tunnel to see if he sees any train lights. To see if a train was approaching shortly.

He looked the other way to see if a train had just left. He saw the back of the train. So, he knew he had just missed a train. That meant there will be no train for a little while.

He walks to the benches on the platform. He figures, he might as well sit down and wait. He looks around, up and down the platform since it was nothing else to do. He looks down the platform, he notices a couple of big cardboard boxes opened.

He thought nothing of it. Living in New York city, you see all type of weird things, in the subway system. He stood when he heard a train coming. But quickly, he realized it was not his train. It was the express train going through the station. He sat back down on the benches.

Out of boredom, he looks back at the cardboard boxes. He saw one of the boxes shake. He rubs his eyes thinking maybe it was just his imagination. But when the box shook again. That is when it caught his attention, for real this time. He thought it might have been a rat, or a strong wind from the trains coming in and going out of the train station, that made the boxes shake on the platform.

He thought less of it. When he thought about what could have made the box shake. Then when he saw a piece of the cardboard box open like a door.

He could not help it, he could not turn away, he had to see what was going on with that. He saw a very tall black man come out the box closest to where he was sitting at. He could not believe what he saw.

He was not surprised, New York City, is known for unexpected and unpredictable moments. The homeless man stood in front of the box, he stretches his arms out and yarns. The man carried on like he was in front of his house. Blinded to everything and everyone who was around him.

He did not care who was watching him, so it seemed. A homeless man living in a cardboard box, on a train platform, classified as being a bum, to the world.

What made everyone take notice, is when the man went to the corner of the platform to urinate. Then the man walks back to his cardboard box, holding a conversation with himself. With all of what everyone on the platform saw, everyone could not wait until the train came.

When the train finally arrived, everyone quickly boarded the train. To be honest, everyone could not wait until the train doors closed. And the train got out of the train station.

What Mike liked about college was the fact, everyone could blend in with the student body. College in general, nobody cared about where you came from, your living conditions, how much money you have. Last, but not least, how you dressed.

Meaning new clothes, used clothes, old clothes was just clothes to all. The professors looked at the class as being a class. Also, if you came to class or if you did not, it was solely up to you. All the focus grownups looked at it the same way, their goal was to get an education, to one day, get further than their current situations.

Some could not comprehend what college was about, obtaining knowledge to add to the knowledge they have already acquired.

The first couple of months went by quickly. The winter, well that was another story. Usual routine, waiting for the train at the train station. He sat down on the platform bench.

He looked to see if the cardboard boxes were still there. This time the other cardboard box started moving. A white man came out of the other box. He went where the other man went to urinate on the platform wall in the corner.

Mike turned his head away like he did the last time. He stood up to look, into the train tunnel to see if the train was on the way. He sat back on the bench; an old lady sat on the bench on the others side of him.

Mike began to smell a cigarette burning. He looks back in that direction to see where the smell was coming from. He saw where the smell was coming from, where the cardboard boxes was located at.

The black bum came out of his cardboard box to ask the white bum, for some of his already lit cigarette. Mike felt a way about homeless bums, in general.

On one hand, he felt like he was a few steps away from being one, himself. Living in a cardboard box, in the same conditions.

He thanked God for his grandmother for taking in him and his sisters. He was aware, if she did not, his sisters would of wind up in the foster care system. And he would have been homeless, probably living in a cardboard box, for real. That was an extremely sensitive spot for him.

While Mike was in his thoughts, and waiting for the train, the big black homeless man began to walk in his direction. The little old lady got scared. Who was next to him on the bench?

So, the young man prepares himself, just in case if he had to defend himself and the old lady. Before he could reach Mike, the man stops at the garbage can on the platform.

He reaches inside the garbage and pulls out a half-eaten sandwich. He broke off the eaten part that had the imprints of teeth marks on it. Then he began to eat the sandwich.

Mike was ready to vomit off what he just saw. The old man looks at Mike, he smiles at him and takes another bite of the sandwich. He turns around and walks back to the cardboard box.

Mike was disgusted from what he just saw. He quickly got up to see if the train was coming. He wanted to get out of there with the quickness. He had no judgement, on what he saw.

It was the way he saw it. That is what had him going. He rode the train that morning more focus, than he ever was about getting a good education. He knew, he did not want to end up like the men he just saw. That was all the motivation he needed. All he knew, he wanted to accelerate and elevate at work and college.

Every evening when he got off work, he picked up some groceries from his job, to take home. A good thing about working at a supermarket, he knew when and what will be on sale prior to the public knowing.

With that knowledge and his employee discount, he learned how to save a lot of money on groceries.

That night he thought about what he saw earlier that morning on the train platform. He felt like no one should live like that, digging in the garbage to get food, to eat. He picked up a bag of rolls and a can of grounded coffee.

He remembers his mother always saying help people in need, even if you are in need yourself. He always made sure he brought things he knew his sisters liked to eat.

While in the kitchen, helping his grandmother with the groceries. He explained to his grandmother what he was trying to do. She liked, what he had planned out to do. She told him to go to the discount store to get some coffee cups and coffee cup lids. He went to purchase what she told him to get.

When he got back home, his grandmother volunteered to prepare the coffee for him. which was good because he was not a coffee drinker, so he did not have a clue on preparing coffee. His grandmother loved the way Mike thought about helping a couple of homeless men.

The next morning, he places the cups of coffee and a butter rolls in two separate paper bags. He took the bags with him, he drops off his sisters, then he went to the train station. He went to the cardboard boxes that was at the end of the platform.

He places each bag next to each cardboard box. When he went to place the bags at the boxes, each man saw what he was doing, so they took the bag from where he placed them at.

He left feeling like he did something for less fortunate people. It felt good because it came from his heart. His good deed of the day. He genuinely believed in, if you do something nice from the heart, without expecting something in return. A higher force will be grateful and gracious enough to bless him with something good and special in his life.

The next day the men were sitting out of their cardboard boxes. Mike was able to hand the cups of coffee and buttered rolls to the homeless men. The two old homeless men were grateful and happy that someone thought enough of them, to bring them something to eat, and drink.

They appreciated the love. One day unannounced to him, while he was about to give the men cups of coffee and rolls. The police officer stops him, to ask him, what was he doing? The question the officer asked the young man caught him off guard?

Clearly, it did not take a brain scientist to figure out what he was about to do? They saw the paper bags with coffee and rolls in them. To make things even worst one of the police officers searched the two brown paper bags the young man was holding.

Which was totally, uncalled for. While this was going on, he could not help but look at the police officers with a puzzled look on his face. He could not understand why they stopped him to ask him what was he doing?

After the police officer finished asking him a bunch of unrelatable questions, they let him go. So, he could do, what he planned to do. He gave the homeless men each a bag. Then he boarded the train, with the police presence, he almost was late for school.

On the train ride to school, he could not believe how the police officers were acting. He learned a valuable lesson that day. He learned that everyone does not have the same compassion, as others like himself did.

Having a heart to do things for others, without expecting something in return, was a rarity, nowadays. People only thought about themselves. It should not have to take a college kid, who was damn near homeless himself, to find the love in his heart to help people.

He was not complaining, it was just an intellectual observation. It was just fascinating to him. Yet it explained a lot.

For one, he could not help but to think, if he were in that predicament, as those homeless men, would anyone give a damn about him?

He also was mature enough not to think about it in that fashion. Because he believed there were still kind-hearted people out there like himself. That will find the kindness in their heart to look out for people who did not have.

He knew everyone was not screwed up in this cold, divided, heartless world, we all live in. Deep down inside, he understood, he must keep on doing what he has been doing.

The following day when he gave the men coffee and buttered rolls. One of the homeless men told him to forget about the police officers. They are simply confused individuals, that all. Not only did that bring reassurance to the young man.

The young man noticed the big black homeless man was as tall, as he was in stature. He also, noticed the man had a vocabulary. Not judging, but he was not expecting him to respond in an articulate manner.

What the old homeless man said, he understood clearly, what he meant by what he said. Afterwards, they all laughed about the whole ordeal.

Chapter 4
Acts of Kindness

Every day, he saw the men at the train station platform. He gave them cups of coffee and buttered rolls. To some people it was kind a weird for a person to take time out, to give the homeless something to eat.

People with common sense understood what the young man was doing. Afterwards, he waited for the train like everyone else. People go off one's outer appearance, never knowing how people inner self looks, like.

Never knowing what is going on in one's mind. They only see the shell of one's body. Mike thoughts were, this could be easily himself, if he did not stay focus on what he had to do, with work and school. He already felt, like he had one foot in one direction, the direction of failure. And the other foot in the direction of success.

It was all about moving his feet in the right direction. As time went on, he discovers, the two homeless men were some interesting characters. He begins to see the human side of them. Something that no one saw in an awfully long time, in these men lives.

Especially the black homeless man they called chief. The other man's name was Norman, but chief called him Pork chop.

One day the train was delayed, due to technical problems. So, everyone was stuck in the station for a while. Mike spent more time on the platform. Chief saw that mike had a book bag on.

When had he questioned Mike about it? Mike told the men, that he was in college. Also, he explains, when they saw him, in the morning, he is on his way to school.

Chief asks him, what was he going to college for? What was his major? Also, what did he want to become? Which all were good questions to ask.

Mike tells them, his plans on his future. He states that one day, he is going to write books for a living. Chief smile at the fact, that he could see the ambition in the young man's eyes.

Chief went on to say, that he has a story tell. That he wanted one day, to be in a book. A story that was passed down generation to generation in his family. A story that his grandfather told him when he was a little boy. His family history.

He explains to the young man, his grandfather told him a story about Indians, living in the south, in peace and harmony.

Until their land got invaded and they were stripped of their land, their identity, their culture, and placed into slavery. Which was an atrocity. Such a sad time in his family history.

The young man did not know what to say about, what he just heard. Pork chop was speechless. Mike's train came. Thank God, the train finally arrived, because if not, he would have been, even more late, than he already was.

Chief tells mike, he had more of that story to tell him. And he will tell him some more of it the next time he sees him. Mike was cool with that. As mike's train left the train station and he was in route to school. Mike thought about it.

Mike knew, and felt, this would be a great story to practice his taking notes skills on, and putting the notes into book form, for him.

One of the keys to becoming a great Author. Plus, he was always ready to hear a great story. A story he did not mind hearing about. It caught the young man's interest, to say, the least.

Chapter 5
Natives
&
Invaders

The next day when mike gave the men coffee and buttered rolls. Chief wanted to know who made the coffee, because who ever made it, knows how to make coffee. Mike laughed, as he told him, his grandmother made the coffee.

While chief was chewing his roll and drinking his coffee, he asked Mike to take out his notebook. He wanted to waste no time, he wanted to get back to the story he wanted to tell. Mike anticipated he was going to say that. So, he already prepared himself. He pulls out his notebook out of his bookbag. He pulls a pen out of his pants pockets. Just like he was in class, ready to get schooled.

Pork chop was ready to hear some more too. Chief began his story explaining how the invaders was able to capture the people of the land, without much blood shed.

How one day, the tribal chief's daughters and the other young women and girls of the tribe went down to the lake to bathe. Just like they always did. The chief always sends a guard or two for protection.

The guards were instructed to watch the women from a far. The guard were mainly there to protect the women from things like wild animals, and things of that nature.

The tribal land was known as a very peaceful land. War was not common among the people. While the women bathe in the lake. The guard secured the perimeter.

Normally, the younger guard would try to take a sneak peak, as the women bathe, in the river. He really liked the chief's eldest daughter, Spirit. Word did get back to Chief Eagle about the invaders from a land they knew nothing of.

How these invaders were power hungry, war loving type of people? Who wanted to take everything in their site? Conquering land was their quest for power.

The chief had his men prepared, just in case if they had to defend their land. That was the last message he received from his brother Chief Hawk, who was the tribal chief of a tribe that was not that far away.

He thought he would have had more time to get prepared. But that was not the case. The guards who were assigned to watch the women of the tribe, roam the perimeter to make sure everything was safe and secure.

The women and girls of tribe was happy, joyful, having a good time.

Washing clothes, bathing, singing tribal songs. One of the guards spotted something that was suspicious lurking through the woods in the forest. He went to investigate his findings. What he saw was a soldier, he never saw before.

Quickly, he ran to warn every one of his findings. But on his way, he did not get far, before the army of invaders cornered him in, out in the forest. They killed the guard.

Then they pursued through the forest. When the other guard went to check on his partner. He was ambushed by a slew of bullets from the invader's army. He had no chance. He was dead on the spot.

As the army of men moved through the forest looking for a village to destroy and take over. As they grew thirsty, they began to search for water as well. That is when one of the men spotted, water and to his surprise, a group of women bathing in the nude.

He could not believe is eyes. He notified the leader of the army of men. He told his men there's water and women over by the river. The men needed and wanted both.

The men attacked the women. They came, so fast, the women were caught off guard. They came so fast only few were able to put back on their clothes. They fought off the men as best as they can.

It gave a little more time, for some more of the women to put some clothes on, before they were totally captured. The leader of the army of men knew, with the large number of women they captured, there must be a village nearby.

He orders his men, not to kill them. His goal was to find the village, so he could conquer and destroy it. He instructed them to lead him and his army to the village. From which, they came from.

Some women died resisting capture. Some soldiers stayed with the women who were fully nude, by the river. Where they continuously raped and tortured, the women left behind. The leader of the army of men forced the other women to take them to the village.

This was the second time he ordered them. With patience running out, he turns around and shoots one of the Indian women in the head, in front of all the women.

Once they realized that the malicious, cruel man in front of them, was willing to kill all of them, if they did not comply with his demands.

At that point, he placed fear in all the women's hearts. Then when one of his men grabbed a little girl and threaten to kill her. Chief Eagle's eldest daughter had seen enough, she had no choice but to take them.

She did not want anyone else to die, including herself. They followed the women into the village. Unannounced to the Chief and his men, the army invaders were already in the heart of the village. With the women and children held at gunpoint.

The chief already knew, he was at a disadvantage. The leader of the army did not hesitate to demand, that the chief relinquish his land to them. He went on to say, surrender or be killed.

At this point, his main concern was the safety of his daughters, the women and children of his tribe. He ordered his tribal men to drop their weapons. And comply with the invaders demands. The Chief did not want any bloodshed.

Clearly, he noticed the type of weapons, the invaders had. Especially, after they saw what the weapon, the invader called a gun could do. The leader of the invaders pulled his gun from his waist and shot one of the Indian men in the chest. He died instantly.

The tribe's eldest chief came outside of his hut to see what was going on. What got his attention was he heard a sound he never heard before. He wanted to see what was going on.

The old chief was very elderly, the father of the current Chief, Chief Eagle. As the army of men saw the old man coming towards them, another man from the army shot the old man.

The loud roar from the sky darkens the village. Tears of thunder poured out of the sky. Blood bled generations and generations of history which was in the old Chief's body.

Chief Eagle fell to his knees to catch his dying father's head and body, so it would not slam to the hard ground. He held his dying father in his arms, as his father dies.

The last thing his father whispered into his son's ears with his dying breath was, never forget this day in history, never forget your people, your ancestors always teach our people their identity to generations to follow.

Because once it is lost, it will be hard to get it back. Who we are and who we were? As death came into a once peaceful village and took the Chief's soul. And left a lifeless body which Chief Eagle held with tears in his eyes.

The nightmare on this day was only the beginning. The Chief was aware of that. The army of invader occupied the land until a group of settlers came to purchase the land.

Within, a few months a wagon full of settlers came. They brought some items with them. Once the settler named Mr. Parker purchased the land. The leader of the army of the invaders and his army left on to another quest to conquer more land.

He did leave several men to make sure the settlers would not be harmed. The settlers moved onto the land like they owned it. They began to chop down trees from the forest. Mr. Parker paid chief to use his men, to help and assist in building the big house on the land.

After the houses were built and the big land of trees were torn down. They laid down seeds as far as the eyes can see. Also, they caught many animals, and they build a huge farmhouse.

Mr. Parker paid them for their services. What the chief thought was not all what he thought it would be.

In fact, what started as a partnership, a treaty quickly turned around into enslavement of the chief's people. The people of the land, who resided on the land which once was their village.

Slavery has been casted down on the peaceful people of this tribe. Not only did they steel their land to build a house, plant crops. But they took their freedom as well.

Mike took down all the notes that chief provided him with. Mike was interested in the story, he wanted to hear more.

The train indicator came on in the train station. Mike began to pack his things back into his bookbag. Chief tells the young man, that he has a whole lot of this story to tell him about. Pork Chop did not know what to say nor how to react to what he just heard.

Even though Mike really wanted to continue. But the train came, and he got on board. They all agreed to carry on about it another day.

Chapter 6
Heartaches

The next day after he gave the men something to eat and drink. Chief continued where he left off at. He went on to talk about how the tribe's Chief did not want any bloodshed if their demands were not met. He did not want the people of the tribe to be divided. Complying was the best way to at least, make sure they can stay together for the most part.

That was most important to him. Foreseeing the darkness in his people's future. He was all too aware of the hell he sees in their near future. He enforces the people of the tribe to follow whatever Master Parker wanted.

Everyone did not agree with the chief's strategy. Especially the Chief's eldest son, young chief. Who was in total outrage with the idea of submitting to those evil, wicked people?

His son wanted to fight to gain the tribe's freedom, and land back. Even though, by this time they were not outnumbered, but they were out gunned.

Chief Eagle told his son to think, before he goes out there and gets everyone killed. Pride is not always the key, when it comes down to survival.

He reminds his son he needs to think about their generations to come. He makes his son understand, if all of them get killed, their bloodline dies as well. The Chief emphases on how important it was for their blood lines to keep flowing.

With all the people of the tribe doing what the Chief wanted them to do. The old village became a thriving plantation. Chief Eagle taught Mr. Parker just about everything Mr. Parker knew about running this land.

He taught him, how to plant the crops, take care of a farm, how to bathe properly, etc. Mr. Parker with the help of the chief, placed all the field slaves at position that caters to each one of their strengths, matching their skill level.

That made production more efficient and faster. As times went on, the slaves became a great asset to Master Parker. He trusted his slaves to carry-out and run just about everything that pertained to the plantation's daily duties.

As the trust grew stronger. He made a few slave men trustees. He authorizes the trustees to go to the town to purchase all the necessities to run the plantation, at its full capacity. Also, sell the products that was grown and made on the Parker's plantation.

Chief Eagle was placed in charged to overlook most of all activities that was related to the plantation. He was not the overseer. Master Parker had a guy named Ed, for that.

But for the most part chief was in charge. By Master Parker making that move, he did not have to worry that much about any slave rebellions or any slaves trying to escape.

The whole tribe was loyal to their chief. On a random day, Master Parker decides to accompany Chief and young Eagle into town. Master Parker had to take care of some business at the bank. He went to deposit a great deal of money.

Chief carried on with getting the supplies for the estate. Master Parker told Chief to drop him and young Eagle off in front of the bank.

While, they were in the bank, the banker said hello to Master Parker. He looked at young Eagle. He told him, "No niggers are allowed in this bank". Then he said, "niggers are not welcomed here!" The banker screamed and told him to get out. Young Eagle looks at Master Parker, to see what Master Parker was going to say about that? Master Parker looks into the young man's eyes. He repeated what the banker said to him.

This was the first time, he ever heard Master Parker call him a nigger. It was not the last time, either. Young Eagle did what the man told him to do. Once he started walking towards the front door. The Bank clerk stopped him. He orders him to go through the back door.

After he states that niggers go out the back way. Then the banker and Master Parker laughed like something was funny? Young Eagle had to walk where there were mud, dog shit, and horse manure. He tries to avoid the debris as much as possible not to step in any of the filth.

He slips on a small pebble and falls, flat on his face in the muddy feces. His clothes were drenched and smelly, he did not want to come out from the back of the bank. He was embarrassed over the whole situation. Chief came back to the bank with the wagon full of supplies. He picked up Master Parker.

He asks, where was young Eagle? Master Parker pointed to the back of the bank, he chuckled as he pointed. Chief went to the back of the bank to find his son. Young Eagle was sitting there in the mud. He quickly went over to pull his son out of the mud. Young Eagle smell was unbearable.

Chief had no choice but to make young Eagle walk home behind the wagon. The young Chief's feelings were way beyond hurt. His anger was unmatched. Chief's eldest son never looked at Master Parker the same ever again.

Young Eagle tries to maintain a somewhat normal life in a place, where he knew not anymore.

Chief finishes with this part of the story on that day. Mike and Pork chop was deep into the story that was being told. They were almost picturing what Chief was explaining to them.

The energy in his words. You could not help but feel. Strength was in every word. Mike left for school. Wondering what is next in this interesting story.

Chapter 7
Psychological warfare

As the days went by, Chief began to get more intense with his story he was telling the young man. Mike and Pork Chop listens on as Chief tells them the story of Master Parker was a very smart manipulative individual.

What made him a genius, was he had his slaves feeling like they had some type of control over what was going on, on the plantation.

He did it, by having different slaves in charge of different things. By doing this, it made Master Parker a very wealthy man.

In a matter of time, he became the richest man in the whole little town where the Parker's plantation was located at. As being the wealthiest family in the town they began to buy and own the town. If they did not own it fully, they had invested in partnerships.

To avoid the town's bank from going bankrupt, the mayor of the town asks Master Parker to buy the bank, so the bank could stay opened. Since he owned most of the money in the bank anyway. For Master Parker everything was going well.

He came to a foreign land and made himself a fortune.

This went on for about a little under a decade, or so. Master Parker was known around the plantation for raping young slave girls and women. He was notorious when it came to sexually assaulting slaves.

He even fathered, quite of few slave's babies. Everyone on the plantation knew about it. Mostly everyone who names did not have Parker to them. Most turned a blind eye towards the criminal atrocities.

Most of the slave women and girls prayed that the old man did not come their way. Master Parker did not care if the slave woman was young, old, fat or skinny.

If he wanted them sexually, he took it whenever, wherever he wanted on the plantation. Which terrified the slave women?

Even worst, the male slaves felt vulnerable when it came to this matter. Chief Eagle's eldest son, young Chief Eagle grew into a very tall, strong physically fit man.

They said the young Chief was strong like a bull. Young Chief's attitude did not change much through the years. The way he felt about Master Parker ways and actions.

He did not trust anything about the old man. One thing the majority, of slaves liked about Master Parker was he was brutally honest. He let it be known, he was an extreme racist scavenger, preying on the helpless slaves he owned.

At times, which can be manageable. Mrs. Parker on the other hand, she came off as being compassionate, caring, peaceful, understanding about the unjust predicament the slaves were facing. She acts like, she was their friend.

Which, everyone in the tribe knew, she was just as cruel as Master Parker, if not worst, especially when she did not get her way. The house slaves had a difference of opinion of the Parkers.

The house slaves really thought and believed the Parkers really cared about them. Like the Parkers were their friends. The relationship between the house slaves and the field slaves divided the tribe.

Mainly, because the house slaves felt like they had something over the field slaves. Genuinely, feeling like they were more important, in return feeling like they were better. Because they were able to wear Master and Mrs. Parker old garments.

The field slaves were issued the house slaves old hand me downs. By the time the clothes got to the field slaves, the clothing was so worn and used, the clothing easily ripped.

Commonly, they all had the upmost respect for the old Chief, and the tribe's elders. Chief's wife and daughters worked in the house.

The story got cut short for the moment due to train delays. The train platform became crowded. Chief did not like crowds.

Once the platform became packed, he went back into his fortress of solitude, his cardboard box.

Mike put his notebook back in his bookbag. He figures, he will tell him some more of this story another day. He understood why Chief did that.

That day Pork Chop did not come out of his box in the first place, because of the crowd.

Chapter 8
The nephew

The next time Mike saw chief, chief asks Mike where did he leave off at? Mike told him. Then Chief continues with his story.

He talked about when Mrs. Parker's nephew from another plantation came to stay for the summer. Dave came along with a couple of his friends. As soon as they arrived, they were mischievous.

These guys were very cruel, racist and evil towards the slaves on the plantation. They started being extremely violent to the slaves who did not do what they said. They did as they pleased. It went from drinking all the alcohols they can stomach. To raping women slaves with brutal force.

If any male or female opposes to what they were doing? It took little to nothing, for them to whip and beat a slave. When Young Chief questioned, the three-man crew about what they were trying to do?

Young Chief overheard the men talking about teaching a young boy slave, a lesson by raping him. Because he was sitting on the steps of the master's house talking to one of Master Parker's daughters.

They did not like the fact, that a little black boy was talking to a little white girl. The little boy and girl were around the same age. They were not even 10 years old at the time. They always talked and played together. They knew each other their whole lives.

It was not anything malice about their friendship. It was normal to everyone who lived on the plantation. Even master Parker did not have a problem with that.

But to strangers to the property, it did not sit well. Rumor on the plantation, was the young boy was one of master Parker's children. He had with an enslaved woman.

While they were drunk sitting by the barn. One of Dave's friends questioned him about a black boy sitting there talking to his little cousin. Dave got angry about it. Young chief was watching, seeing how it all was about to go down, from a far.

When the little girl went into the house. The young black boy walked back to the slave's quarters. On the way to the slave's quarters, the men cornered the young black boy. The young boy had nowhere to run to. They began to beat on him. One of the men pulled down the young boy's pants.

Before it could get any further, Young Chief stopped them from doing, what they set out to do. Young Chief saved the young boy. Which was good and all.

But the repercussions he paid for that action, left him in a whole world of trouble. Because of what he did, he received a vicious beating with the whip.

So brutal, it left Young Chief with broken ribs and a scar they gave him that he would have for the rest of his life. He almost died that day, from the beating. They only reason why they did not get the chance to killed him, was because the little boy went and got the Chief. And Chief went and got Master Parker, to stop them.

Master Parker, the chief, a group of slaves, just about everyone on the plantation came to witness this brutal attack, next to the barn. Master Parker watched for a while. He looked right into Young Chief's eyes. Young Chief stare back, though his vision was bleary from the tears of pain. Then Master Parker smiles and chuckles.

Eventually, he gets his nephew and friends to stop. Young Eagle was badly hurt and bruised for an exceedingly long time. It took months to heal properly. Another day, another reason for Young Chief to despise and dislike, Master Parker.

After a while, even Master Parker grew tired of his nephew and his friends' antics. Everyone was happy when the summer ended. Dave's friend came to the plantation to pick Dave and his buddies up. In his wagon, he had 4 imported African slaves he purchased. Dave asks his uncle to purchase the slaves from his friend.

After, Dave pulled Master Parker to the side to explain that they needed the money to get home. Master Parker purchased the 4 slaves from his nephew. The African slaves was placed with the rest of the slaves on the plantation.

Master Parker and the plantation's overseer gave the new slaves names. They whipped them, until they responded to their new names. They did that to the Indians when they first arrived at the tribe's village, which was now the plantation.

Young Eagle's name given to him was Robert Greenland. Behind the master's back, the slaves still called each other by their tribal names. Young Eagle hated to answer to the name Robert when master Parker called him that. He did not like it at all. He found it to be very disrespectful and degrading.

Mike and Pork Chop stood there in silence while Chief told this part of the story. Before Mike got on the train. Chief asked the young man did he have all of that written down? He just wanted to make sure.

Mike smiled and told him, he got it. His thoughts on the story, he was hearing, was damn, this story was interesting.

Chapter 9
The Africans

The young Chief was already not agreeing with all that has happened. He kept his true feelings to himself. Out of respect to his father, the Chief.

Young Eagle was sitting in the field with his sister Spirit. She tells him, she is thinking about running away, from the plantation.

That thought never crossed his mind. He had to admit that to her. He never thought about it before. She explains to him, that none of the people from a far knows their land better than them. He agrees to her point, she was making. Not with most of what she was saying, out of fear for her life.

In his mind, he felt like why they should have to run away from the land their ancestors occupied for centuries. Running away, just did not make any sense to him.

One of the African slaves tried to run away. They tried to warn him, not to do it that way. But he did not listen to them. He went on and did his own thing. He did not make it that far, when he realized, he did not know the landscape, nor where he was at?

Instead, he just got lost, in the forest. He ran into a runaway slave patrol unit. After they whip him, they brought him back to the plantation. They arrived on the plantation with a horse and a wagon, with the slave being dragged by a chain that was chained to his wrist, connected to the wagon. It was a horrific vision to see.

Being dragged through-out the forest, you think it will be enough, as far as torture goes? But it was not, later that night on the plantation, the overseer decided to give the African slave a whipping of his own.

All through-out the night, while the other slaves were in their slaves' quarters, trying to get some sleep. They could not because all they could hear was the whip lashing to an already torn open back of bare skin.

The loud roar, from the slave man came from the excruciating pain, that was felt. That was not a good night on the Parker's plantation.

Young Eagle and Spirit spoke about that night, the next morning. Spirit was still persistent about what she wanted to do.

She eludes, to the fact, the African man was not from here. That is why he got caught. She did make a valid point. Young Eagle had to acknowledge that.

Since he knew, his sister was going to do, what she wanted to do. All he could do, was tell her to think about what she is going to do, thoroughly. Make sure she plans for a safe getaway. Before she goes for it. She understood and agreed with what her brother was talking about.

A couple of evenings later, Master Parker raped one of the African women. Everyone heard her screaming, fighting off her attacker. No one helped. They all pretended not to hear a thing. So, the woman's screams became whispers into the dark air, of the night.

Not seeing the slave woman for months. When they saw her again, they noticed she was pregnant and showing? Some felt bad about what had happened to her. That quickly changed when she started acting like she was better than everyone else. Because Master Parker gave her light work to do.

She thought, she had some power over the other slaves. Because she was carrying a secret baby by the Master.

Little did she know. Master Parker did that with every enslaved woman he got pregnant. With the attitude she projected, they felt like, it was good for her, what had happened to her. They knew it was all a matter of time before she gets her rude awakening. Right now, she does not understand, she is going to remain a slave.

All the women of the plantation, knew fully, it could be anyone of them next. Unless he already did. Master Parker gave his plantation overseer, more power to run the plantation.

At this point, Master Parker did not always gain knowledge of what went on, on the plantation. After being warned several times, about trying to escape. The African man tries yet again, to escape.

That was the last time, he will ever try to run away. When they caught him this time, after they brought him back to the plantation. From fear of the other slaves thinking they could run away too. The overseer decides to hang the African slave in front of the slave quarters, in the field.

So, everyone could see this as a warning, if anyone of them tries to run away, this too, could be their fate.

Seeing that placed fear in many slave's hearts. This was around the time when the civil war started. Mr. Parker was way too old to fight in the confederate army. Master parker's son was too young to go, as well. His nephew stopped by, to tell his uncle that he was going.

Master Parker's overseer and crew that watched over the slaves went to fight for the confederate army. Only a handful stayed back. Another time and day, that had Young Eagle outraged, to the point, or he could not take it anymore. The day Master Parker raped his baby sister, that was only 12 years old.

While his father was clearly upset behind it. Still his father told them not to react. The Young chief swore revenge one day, over what this wicked man has done. What Master Parker has done to him, his family and his people, who we are all enslaved, because of this evil man.

One day, he promised, he will have his revenge that he seeks. Young chief jumped the broom with one of the elders of the tribe daughters. That was the happiest day in Young Eagle's life. By far, he did not have a smile on his face ever since, their village got invaded.

That day and the love, he has for his wife took him away from the hell, that was all around them. It was like paradise in hell, he once quoted about that day.

Chief stops the story right there for the day. He knew Mike had to get to school. Pork Chop sat there quiet. Mike got on the train wanting to hear more of this great story. He knew, he probably be saying that every time, but he could not help it, that is how he felt about it.

Before Mike left, he did tell the men, Happy Thanksgivings. Chief told Mike, his grandfather used to say, them people were happy taking something that was not given to them.

Mike never thought about it, but everyone has their own opinion about it. The story was the homeless man's story and not Mike's. Mike went on to his college classes, as normal.

Chapter 10
The New Chief

Everything was about to change when the great Chief Eagle became seriously ill. While on his death bed, he placed his eldest son, as the new chief of the tribe. Young Eagle/ Young Chief was now known as Chief Eagle. As it was written in stone, as in tradition.

The lineage of the ancestors was the eldest son of the presiding Chief will one day become chief, and his first-born son will become Young Chief. This practice has gone on in their family history for centuries.

The old Chief wanted Eagle to promise him, he will teach the ways of the ancestors to generations to come and beyond. Also, to listen and accept Master Parker's ways and actions. For the protection of the people of the tribe. Finally, he wanted Eagle to think before he makes any moves. And a move without a thought, is a dumb move to be made.

The new Chief promised his father that he will always be loyal to his father and their tribe. The next morning the old chief dies. Chief wanted to bury his father down by the lake, where they buried all the ancestors at. They been doing this for an eternity.

At first Master Parker did not want Eagle to bury his father by the lake. Due to the fact, that his children played by the lake, and at times, they play in the water of the lake. Eagle felt like Master Parker was overstepping his boundaries.

Eagle felt disrespected when Master Parker suggested, they bury the old Chief in the corn field, in the back of the plantation.

Eagle discusses it with his mother, mother Chief went to Mrs. Parker over this matter. Mother Chief knew her son was going to bury his father in the ancestral grave site, anyway.

To stop bloodshed, she went to the next possible person, who was at least, somewhat reasonable. Mrs. Parker granted them permission to bury the chief by the lake, like their ancestor always did. Eagle questioned about the permission part. She tells him, sometimes you must think. To get your way.

He could not say too much about that, because it worked. They did get their way. By then, the new Chief of the tribe, was looking at things much differently than his father, the old Chief. He always did.

The hatred he processed over the things, he endured, from this whole ordeal. He had a valid reason to feel the way, he felt.

Mike sat there, listening from the platform bench. While Chief and Pork Chop sat on the floor next to the platform bench. Mike wrote all that was said down. Pork Chop was intrigued by the story.

He states, the story keeps on getting better, and better. Mike heard the train indicator. He knew it was time to pack up, his notebook and pen back into his backpack. The train was coming.

The old man tells the young man, he will see him tomorrow. The young man agrees on that plan. Mike boarded his train. The train left the train station. After the sound of the train left the station.

Pork Chop turns to Chief and asks him, was all that mumbo, jumbo he talked about was it really, true? Before Chief could reply, Pork Chop, went on to say, no, it was too good to be true.

Chief tells Pork Chop, to kiss his black ass! They paused, then they both laughed.

Pork Chop picked up, a half-used cigarette clip off the ground, on the platform floor. Someone must have dropped the half of a cigarette. He really did not care, where it came from? He lights the cigarette up and began to smoke.

Chief notices Pork Chop was smoking, he asks Pork Chop to save him some, that's when Pork Chop told him to kiss his white ass. Chief tells Pork Chop, that his ass was so dirty, his ass was probably as black as his by now.

They both laugh as Pork Chop took a couple more pulls of the cigarette before he passes the cigarette over to chief. They always joked with one another like that.

People on the platform, who was waiting for the train, found it odd to see them there. Most stared looking at the homeless men, as being crazy. Sitting in front of human size cardboards boxes, like they were sitting in front of their houses. Which was located at the end of the platform stairs where there was just a train exit, or if you had a token to have access to the train platform.

Where no train station clerk was located at. People who walked pass the homeless men, coming into the subway or leaving the subway, held their noses, trying not to absorb the horrific, unpleasant smell that came reaping off the men's dirty clothes and unbathed skin.

As they looked down at the old homeless men, who were sitting on the platform floor. The old men looked at them like they had the problem, not them. Some people walked past them, calling them bums. They did not care about what anyone thought of them. They just kept on living. Nothing more, nothing less.

Chapter 11

Freedom Run

Master Parker grew old in age. But that did not stop him from raping the girls and women slaves on the plantation. The new Chief grew older, wiser as a man, as time passes on by. He was not nowhere near as old as Master Parker.

In fact, the old master was old enough to be his father. Chief Eagle was in his middle to late 30's. He had children of his own. Things he uses and cherish at times, a lot of it came from what he learned from the wisdom of his father, the old chief. Applying the lessons, making sure all the children of the tribe knew the tribal history.

So, their story of their people will never die out. Eagle had a son, his first born. As he began to walk, talk and understand, they began to call him young Chief like tradition states.

This young Eagle will eventually be the homeless man Chief's grandfather. Master Parker's children grew up too, into young adults. The ones he had with his wife. And the ones he fathered from enslaved women on the plantation.

The ones, he will always deny for the rest his life. Chief watched and watched, he realized, master Parker's children does not have any heart.

They feared bugs and small animals. He knew, he did not have to worry about them, when it is time for him to get his revenge on what has been taking from his tribe. They were weak when it came, to war-like things.

Mrs. Parker never thought to learn the business part of running a plantation of the size of the one they lived on. She always felt like, running daily operations on the plantation was men's work.

She normally invited company over to their big house. To have tea with other slave owner's wives. Or watch the house slaves, making sure everything has done to her satisfaction.

Since, there were not too many white men in their little town, due to most of them was off to fight in the civil war. Besides the elderly and wounded soldiers who came back from the war.

No one was there to stop anything from happening. Eagle's sister Spirit felt this was the perfect opportunity to make a run for it. She took some women and some men with her. They left into the darkness of the night.

She told Eagle, she was going to follow the northern star, north like their father used to tell them, when they were children. That was the last time, the Chief saw his sister. He wished her well, on her journey towards freedom.

Master Parker was outraged that some of his slaves escaped. But it was not too much, he could do about that. He asks Robert about it. Chief responds saying he did not have a clue. Chief did mention that he overheard them saying that they were going south.

He said, what he said to throw Master Parker off their trail. He had the old master thinking the escaped slaves were going south. While all along, Chief was aware they were going north. After complaining about it.

Master Parker states to all, of the other slaves, if the ones who escape get caught, or come back they will be dealt with, in the worst way. All the other slaves knew and understood, what he meant by that.

Chief Eagle turns his back and walks away from Master Parker with a smile on his face. He goes back into the field to complete his daily work on the plantation.

Eagle's wife runs across the field to go and get Eagle. She explains to him, that his mother was terribly ill, and she wanted to see him. Eagle rushes to her bedside. His elderly mother begins to tell him things he did not know about.

She tells him, that Master Parker raped her before. Then he raped Spirit. He took away her innocence. She mentions, that was the main reason why Spirit wanted to run away from the plantation.

He was not shocked nor surprised at anything when it came to Master Parker. It all made sense to the Chief now, that was the reason why his sister was, so head strung on leaving the plantation.

Now, he understood why she wanted to get away. Eagle already made up his mind a long time ago. All he needed was a window of opportunity, to show the world, how he really felt about Master Parker, once and for all.

His mother regained her strength, for the moment. He thanked the ancestors for that. What ignited the spark of fire in Eagle's eyes was when he found out that Master Parker raped his eldest daughter Malwee.

Eagle was as far, as a man can be pushed. The only thing that saved the day, was Eagle's wife gave birth to a baby boy. Which took, Eagle's mind off, of what was at hand.

Mike looked at Chief and Pork Chop too. They wondered why Chief paused at that part of the story, he was telling. Neither one of them knew why, but it was clear to see, chief was speaking with raw feelings about this part of the story.

Mike needed to know why? So, he asked the old man. He wanted to know why Chief got so emotional, at this point of the story. Chief looks at the young man eye to eye, he tells him, chief Eagle's oldest son was his grandfather.

Before the homeless man states that, Mike thought it was just some random story this man was making up in his head. Some folk-story that was passed down generation to generation.

The realization of this man that was before is eyes was a grandson of a man who was born on a plantation. That was mind blowing for the young man to digest. He never viewed it as being a couple generations prior.

Mike was learning so much. So many things he never thought about, to be honest. After Chief said, what he had to say, Chief did not want to talk about it anymore, for the moment.

Mike understood it, he surely did not want Chief to feel any pressure about expressing his family history.

One thing Mike did not express, was the fact, he did not know his own family history. Chief tells the young man they could start off, where they left off at, tomorrow. Mike was okay with that. Chief went back into his cardboard box.

Mike walked away to the middle of the platform, to wait for his train. He knew Chief wanted to be left alone. Plus, to be honest, the smell of the homeless men, can only be tolerated for a short moment of time. Before the smell overwhelms you.

Besides providing coffee and buttered rolls, and hearing Chief's story, Mike did not want to be nowhere near the cardboard boxes.

Chapter 12
Vengeful

As the civil war got more intense. More men, from the little town went off to fight with the confederate army, in the civil war.

While this was happening, many plantations were left for the wives, widowers, other women, the elderly and wounded soldiers to run the business of the plantations.

Eagle knew this was his perfect opportunity to strike. Eagle begins to plot on how to get rid of Master Parker. Something he wanted to do ever since he was a little boy.

He wanted it to be quiet as possible, without any of the other slave masters knowing about it. He was aware he had a small window of an opportunity to pull it off.

The time became, now or never. After months of thinking about it, how to get away with this difficult task that was at hand. He knew if the attempt does not work out in his favor. He surely knew, he would be killed for his actions. He finally came up with the right plan.

The plan was kept a secret from everyone, except the parties that were going to be involved. Only, him and his brothers knew about it.

At this time, Master Parker was obsessed with giving Eagle a hard way to go. This came from as far back, as Eagle's childhood. Everyone knew about it. Master Parker did not like the fact, that the Old Chief left Eagle in charge to take over his position, on the plantation. Being the leader of the slaves.

Master Parker forgot it was not up to him, who was going to be the leader of their tribe. Yes, he could appoint someone to be, in charge of the slaves on his plantation.

To be spiteful, Master Parker places the only African slave man in charge. He made this move, thinking everything would be only business, and not personal. The African man quickly changed his whole demeanor with this position.

He began to walk around the plantation giving orders like he owned it. Like he was Master Parker, himself. He was the definition of losing yourself in a position. He began to think he was better than the natives of the actual land, he resided on.

Every once and a while, even Master Parker questioned him about what he was doing. Also, to remind him, he was a slave too.

Any and everything that went on the plantation, the African slave made sure he reported it. So, Master Parker could know about it. He was loyal to Master Parker. He would do anything for his Master.

Eagle still was in charge to go to town, to pick up supplies and goods for the plantation. The African slave knew nothing about that, he did not even really know where he was at. Let alone, having the knowledge on how to get to town. Master Parker had no choice, but to keep Eagle doing those type of things.

Mainly, because the African slave did not know how to read nor write. Eagle was taught how to read as a child from the overseer's wife. She taught a few of them, not all of them. Because he was one of the chief's children, she taught him.

Also, Eagle was the only one capable of transporting Master Parker, wherever he wanted to go. Eagle knew how to use a horse and a carriage. Not too many slaves on the plantation knew how to do that. Eagle learned from a young boy how to do that. He was taught by his father, the old chief. Master Parker could not deny the fact, that Eagle was very skillful in so many things.

Eagle's mother was up and around, as usual. Which was a good sign for the elderly old Mother Chief of the tribe. Everyone was happy about that. Eagle and his brothers knew that Master Parker had a huge sexual appetite.

Master Parker always lurked at night, roaming the plantation to find a slave to rape. On this night, he found a light skinned slave girl, to rape. He forced her into the barn. He began to rip her clothes off her body, until she was fully nude.

When she would not lay down, he struck her in the face, knocking her down to the ground. Little to Master Parker's knowledge, Eagle and his brothers were waiting in the barn for him. They hid behind the big bundles of hay.

It all happened so fast and quiet. No sounds were made by the Indian men. Until it was time to strike. Master Parker pins the girl to the ground. As he took off his pants. That is when they made their move. Master Parker got caught, literally with his pants down to his knees.

The young half-white slave girl was happy to be saved from being raped. They instructed the young slave girl to leave the barn.

Also, to never speak about this day, for the rest of her life. She promised, she would not. The men murdered Master Parker.

While Master Parker was dying a slow painful death. Chief Eagle stood above him, looking right into his eyes. He tells Master Parker, this was for all the things, he has put his tribal people through.

The taste of revenge was casted upon Eagle's heart and soul. It was finally his. Master Parker died shortly afterwards.

The next morning a couple of slaves, who was assigned to clean the barn, discovers the old master's lifeless body, on the ground.

Mike train was on its way. He mentions to Chief that Eagle finally got his revenge. Chief explains, to the young man, that was not the way the story ends.

Come tomorrow to hear some more of the story. Chief talks about this were only the beginning of the story. There was so much more to the story. Mike could not wait to hear some more.

Chapter 13
Landscape

After the murder of Master Parker. Mrs. Parker wanted to bury the old master secretly. She did not like all the attention, that would have taken place, if word got out that Master Parker got murdered. She did not want everyone, in her business. She ordered the slaves to bury Master Parker outback in the back yard of the master's house.

She understood, at the time they lived in. In history, they did not like a woman owning a plantation, the size of the Parker's plantation. So out of fear, she did not want to lose the plantation. She chooses not to tell anyone.

Since her son was not old enough to take over at the time. Also, her son did not know anything about the plantation, nor the knowledge of running the business that pertain to the daily operations of the plantation. Her plans were to run the plantation as if her husband were still alive.

At least until her son becomes of age, to take over in his father's place. She places Eagle back in charge of everything. Since he knew the most about everything that has to do with the plantation. All the slaves wanted their Chief to be in charge to begin with. She instructs her son to learn how to run the plantation from Eagle.

The African slave warn Mrs. Parker, he felt placing Eagle in charge, would not be such a good idea. She reminds him, that Eagle grew up on this plantation, not him. Plus, what she wants, is what it shall be. The African man got angry over the fact. He was mad over the notion of Chief being in charge, of everyone.

Mostly because he would oversee him. The African man became difficult to work with. He carries on, like he had options. Totally, blind to the fact, that he was a slave on a slave plantation.

Eagle came up with a great idea, that he gave to the African. He tells him, if that was him, and if he felt a certain way about what was going on. And he knew it was not for him, he would leave, and just run away.

The African agrees with chief. He said, maybe that is what he will do. He decides to escape with one of the African women, he came on the slave boat with. They ran away the following day.

He thought he knew it all. Also, he had it all together. Once he, his companion and a couple of other slaves, left the grounds of the plantation.

He got lost. He did not know where he was at, or where he should go? He went South. Which was an awfully bad choice to have made. They walked right into a confederate army camp.

The men saw them lost in the woods. They circled the camp, quite a few times. Until they got spotted. They apprehended him and the other runaway slaves, that followed him into the woods. They told the runaway slaves to surrender.

The African slave thought he could fight his way through the army of men. Once he swung on one of the soldiers. Quickly, he realizes that too, was not a smart move to make. The soldier he swung at, ducked to avoid contact.

Then the soldier pulled out his shot gun, and shot the African slave in the head, from point blank range. He died right there on the spot. The army of men rounded up the rest of the runaway slaves.

The slaves gave up after they saw what happened to the African slave. They placed the body of the dead slave in the wagon. They chain all the runaway slaves together. They made their way towards the Parker's plantation.

The runaway slaves followed the wagon back to the plantation, under heavy army presence. They arrived at the Parker's plantation. Eagle spotted them from a far while he was painting the fences of the plantation.

Once they got close enough, Eagle is opening the gates to let the confederate army through, into the Parker plantation. They tell Eagle to go and fetch Master Parker for them.

Eagle had to think sharply on his feet. He tells the leader of the unit that Master Parker was not there, now. He suggests, they take the runaways slaves and wagon to the master's house where Mrs. Parker was at.

The unit follows Eagle deeper inside the plantation grounds. He led the army of men to the master's house. While the army waited outside. Eagle goes inside to get Mrs. Parker. He tells her, what was going on, as far as he knew.

Mrs. Parker came outside to greet the army. Eagle began to talk about how Master Parker went away on a business trip. He says it enough times, so Mrs. Parker could catch on to the story he was trying to tell.

She tells the army of men, that they could turn over the runaway slaves to her. She lets them know the runaway slaves will be dealt with. Eagle takes the chained runaway slaves away as instructed. He takes them out to the back of the barn. Out of sight, of the confederate army unit.

The highest ranked soldier asked again about Master Parker. She said the same thing as Eagle told them. That he was away on business. One of the soldiers wanted to know, what she wanted to do with the dead runaway slave's body.

They explain their actions, they told her the truth about it. They told her about how the African slave tried to attack one of them. They had no choice but to defend themselves.

Which resulted in, the killing of the runaway slave. She looks in the wagon, to identify the dead body. She discovered it was the African slave man. She just shook her head, in disbelief. She did not even realize that he had ran away. She orders a group of male slaves to take the body to the corn field. Where he will be buried at shortly.

The leader of the unit, wanted to know which direction did Master Parker travel to? He wanted to know because he was concerned about the safety of the old master.

He went on to say, they were losing the Civil war. So, traveling north at this time, would not be such a good idea. She responds, saying to her knowledge, the old master was traveling south. Mrs. Parker thanked the Confederate Army for bringing her runaway slaves back.

After the army left, she calls Eagle to her. She tells him what she wanted the runaway slaves to do. Eagle unchained the runaway slaves, he told them to grab some shovels. Their punishment was to bury the dead African slave, whom they tried to run away with.

By making the runaways do that, it was a learning lesson behind it, being taught. It was up to the individual slave to understand it. Simple, if you try to run away again this could be you next time.

Chapter 14
A dying Request

This day Mike decides to go to the neighborhood bodega to buy the men a couple lucy's. Which is a cigarette sold separately. He gave each man a cigarette along with a cup of coffee, with a buttered roll.

He places it in their individual bag. Pork Chop discovers his first. He was so happy, he turned red. He tells Mike, he has not had a whole brand-new cigarette in years.

He was about to light his cigarette up. Until Chief advises him not to do so. Chief wanted them to save their cigarettes for later. After Chief takes a bite of his buttered roll and washes it down with some hot coffee.

Mike takes out his notebook out of his backpack. He reaches and pulls out his pen from his front pants pocket. While Chief ate a little more of his roll. Then chief went back into telling his story.

Mrs. Parker knew how hard the workers, work during this hard, difficult time for her and her family. She always valued her friendship with the old Mother Chief. They been on the plantation so long, they practically raised their children together.

In fact, Mother Chief was her children's nanny. She raises the Parker's children from birth. She nurtured the Parker's babies. She was like an indirect second mother to the children. Yes, Mother Chief was classified as a slave woman.

But the Parkers' and their children look at her beyond labels. Not only did she do that. She also cooked the food they ate. She supervised the other house slaves. When she grew ill, this time. She knew, she was dying. She asks for one request.

She asks Mrs. Parker, could she be kind enough to give her children some land? Mrs. Parker wrote it in her will. She gave Mother Chief's children the land that the slave quarters were on. To Mrs. Parker, it was not a lot, but a promise she made. That she wanted to keep.

That made Mother Chief an incredibly happy woman, beyond the circumstances. Mother Chief dies shortly afterwards. Chief Eagle was granted permission to bury his mother in their ancestry bury grounds by the river on the planation.

During this time in history, the confederate army lost the civil war. They were retreating, back to the south, back to their little hometowns.

The union was shortly behind them. Every town the Union army enters, baring the good news for the enslaved peoples of America. The news they delivered was President Lincoln had freed the slaves. A new day in the South was born. The sun began to shine again. Which it brought light to a place that was dark for decades.

Eagle receives the news. It was bittersweet for him. All the other former slave cheered the union army on. They celebrated the freedom that was cast upon them again.

Eagle still had his doubts, about what they meant by freedom. Knowing his oppressors like he did. He wanted to see what was going to be next. He also was nobody's fool. Mrs. Parker passes away that same evening. No one knew the cause. The doctor said, she died of a heart attack in her sleep. The Parker children did not know what to do with a plantation of ex-slaves.

Many slaves with their newfound freedom travelled north. Never to returned to the south ever again. The Parker's children came up with an idea, if any ex-slaves wanted to leave their property, they can. For the ones who wanted to stay at their free will, they will be compensated for their services.

Also, they can continue to live in the slave quarters, for free. But they had to take care of the slave quarters themselves. Mr. Parker explains, all of this to Chief Eagle. Eagle agrees with mostly all of what the young Mr. Parker was saying. But he had a couple of things, they had to go over.

First, Eagle wanted to tear down the slave quarters and build house on the same piece of land. He was not asking, he was, telling, the young man his plans. What him and his people of his tribe was going to do with the land that was promised to them from Mrs. Parker. Even though they knew the land was theirs to begin with.

But Chief Eagle wanted to stroke the young man ego a little bit. Eagle knew he needed help funding his project. He wanted a start-up money loan, for building material supplies.

Andrew, the son of Master Parker, always looked up to Eagle. He was like one of his childhood heroes. He kept his respect for Eagle at the highest regards. Without much being asked, he offers to fund the Chief's project, building houses in place of the slave quarters. Andrew knew he still needed people to work at the plantation. Mainly, the ex-slaves who have been running it for years.

Since, he needed workers to work the field. He hires the men of the tribe as sharecroppers. Eagle vows to always stay on his tribal land. He got some of his people's land back. The area the slave quarter was built on.

Once they torn down the old slave's quarters, they noticed, it was much more land space behind the slave quarters. That was part of the parker's plantation that the parkers did not know about. The piece of land was connected to where the slave quarters was at, that led down past the tribal burial site, all the way to the river.

What happened was Mrs. Parker did not know too much about land mass and length. If she knew what she was giving up to the slaves at the time, she would not had signed over that much land.

Just like that, chief and his tribe triple their land, they owned. When Andrew found out about the discrepancy of what his mother thought she gave the now ex-slaves. He did not care too much about it.

Because when his father was the slave master, the family became so wealthy that it did not bother him at all. Truly he was happy for Chief and his tribe.

Andrew did not share the same views as his father did. He did not look at the people as slaves or ex-slaves, but he did not consider them equal to him or his race.

Eagle knew it was a blessing from the ancestors. By law, Chief Eagle owned a large portion of the plantation. Not as much as Andrew. Andrew still owned the majority. Eagle was happy about that. But he really wanted to get all their land back, one day.

Andrew continues to live in the master's house. Where his parents once lived at. And where he grew up at. Chief Eagle and the men of his tribe built themselves houses.

House by house until it looked like a little town of their own. They build a town store on their property. To serve the people of the village, so they would not have to go in town, where there were extremely racist people at.

Eagle purchases a lot of things from Andrew. Things that the plantation produced. Like dairy, fruit and vegetables, etc. He places in his store. After President Lincoln's assassination things change, but more things were more like normal again, in the south.

Just like the Chief anticipated it would be. Everything was going well as they could be. Spirit was able to send a letter back home. Eagle receives the letter in the mail. That was the first time Eagle had anything ever mailed to him.

On the outside, it was addressed to Robert Greenland, which everyone who knew him, knew that he hated that name. But that was his government name, that was given to him. He opens the envelope. He takes the paper out in it. He sees it was a letter from his sister Spirit. He tells his brother Buck about what he has received.

Buck was happy to hear about it. He wanted to know what she was saying in the letter. Eagle, Buck, Spirit and the rest of the Chief children was taught how to read and write on the plantation when they were children. He gathers all the people of the tribe together, to hear the letter Spirit sent.

He read it out loud, for the ones who could not read. She talks about how the North was much different than the South, in so many ways. She explains, how the North had cities to live in. Beautiful tall buildings, trains, cars and factories.

She tells them, she met a wonderful man. She got married and now she has some children of her own. She states she was happy and working a good job. She stresses the fact, that she got paid to work.

She talks about how her husband has a lot of money. They live in a great apartment building. She also let the people of her tribe know, if anyone of their tribal family wanted to come to New York City and stay with her and family until they get off their feet, they are more than welcome. Even if they wanted to come for a short period of time, just to visit.

She does mention, she really missed everyone. Her letter to the family was very-heartwarming. Eagle was excited to know his sister made it. And she was safe and sound.

After hearing the letter, some of the people of the tribe decided to take up Spirit's offer. They packed their things and headed north to Harlem, in New York City to meet up with Spirit.

Eagle understood the reason, why some wanted to get away from this place. They feel like it would be better than being in this racist town.

Where there were limitations on what people of color could do or achieve. People felt stagnated. Living a place that has racism embedded in the core of it. Most people just wanted to live a free life.

Eagle also knew many had to stay on their tribe's property. The ones who left. Left with the blessings of the Chief. His eldest daughter left with the group. He told his daughter to be safe. And when she reaches her aunt Spirit, she should write him a letter. He wanted to make sure she makes it up there safely. His daughter promised she would do that.

While the men of the tribe were building more and more houses, on the land. They built a school for the children of the tribe. The school was to teach the kids how to read and write. But to also teach them about their heritage and culture.

Where the slave quarters were, now looked like a little town of their own. Eagle went into town, to open a bank account. To his surprise, the same bank teller he saw years ago, was still working there. The teller could barely recognize Eagle.

He grew in every way possible since then. Even though the Parker's own the bank he was at. The bank clerk refuses to do business with him. After Eagle shows him a great deal of money in cash.

The bank teller tells his assistant to go and get the sheriff of the town. The sheriff arrested Eagle thinking he stole the money. They were not used to seeing someone of his kind with that type of money. That is what was said.

They confiscated his money and put him in the town's jail. He sat there for a couple of days. Until Andrew heard somebody at the bank talking about it. Andrew questions the teller about it. Andrew got Eagle's money back.

Then he went to straighten out the details with the sheriff of the town. Once Andrew explains it to the sheriff. Eagle was released from jail. Eagle deposits his money in the Parker's bank, with the help of Mr. Parker. Eagle suggested to Andrew, that he should open a bank in their new town, they were building. Eagle reminds Andrew that money was just money, it has no color to it.

Andrew thought about it. He agrees with him. Plus, he saw the difficulty it was for people of color to bank in town.

By giving them their own bank which he would own, would be profitable for him as well. Everyone in the town knew blacks trying to open bank accounts in the town was a no-no. In that little town all it took was something being said or done. The place was waiting to erupt. Anything would ignite total hell and chaos in town.

Like when a young black boy from another plantation waved Hello, to a white girl in town. He did not verbally spoke to the girl. He did not say a single word out of his mouth. Still a hand wave was a big enough thing for the locals of the town, to be in an uproar about it.

The next time anyone saw the boy. They saw him, hung dead with a savagely beaten body, hanging on the town's flagpole. Where everyone could view. That is what they called southern justice, in the south.

whoever did it, wanted to see the remains of this young black boy. The young girl Master Parker was trying to rape, the day he got murdered. She grew into an incredibly attractive young woman.

Due to her complexion, she could almost pass for white. Rumor on the plantation was that Master Parker was the young lady's father.

From one of the enslaved women, he raped almost two decades ago. He must have forgot, or he just did not care. Because truth be told, he was trying to rape his own daughter. If he did not get stopped.

While in town she meets a white man named Ralph. He pursued her, even though you could tell she was mixed. He did not care because of her shade. He wanted to have her. Somewhere down the line after a couple of nights of passion. Ralph falls in love with Lilly.

He goes on to tell her, she could tell him anything, and everything. He wanted to know it all. After she got pregnant by him, she begins to tell him all about her past. She did it thinking, she would be more accepted. She was too white to be black, and too black to be white.

Confusion, she defines the word. She talks about what her mother told her when she asked her who her father was? At first, for years, whenever she asked her that question, she looks at her and cries.

But after years and years of avoiding answering the question. Her mother finally told her the truth. Her mother was raped by Master parker.

And that is how she was conceived. He already knew she was part black. How she got her white side was the kicker.

Then, what she said next, made her story even more troublesome. She went on to talk about the night Master Parker tried to rape her in the barn on the Parker's plantation. Ralph asked her, to say what she just said again. He wanted to make sure, what he thought he just heard. He wanted to get that part straight, that her own father tried to rape her.

That was way too deep for Ralph to comprehend. At first the story she was telling him, felt untrue. By looking into her eyes, he could tell she was telling the truth. She tells him, the only reason why Master Parker failed on raping her was because a group of tall slave men saved her.

After stopping Master Parker from raping her, the men told her to leave the barn. That was the last time, she saw Master Parker alive. After Ralph thought about it for a little while, about what she was saying?

He came with his conclusion, that these slaves, she was talking about, murdered Master Parker.

Before he goes and tells his close friend Andrew about his findings. He chooses to see if he could eventually get some name out of her. For now, he will just keep all of this to himself. Knowing Master Parker was murdered by slaves, the only question that was left, was who?

After Chief finishes up telling this part of the story. Pork Chop was already smoking his cigarette. Chief asks him to save him some. Mike was stunned with the story. Pork Chop smoke quietly far, but near enough to hear the story.

They both saw the look on Chief face. His facial expression could tell it all. The train indicator came on in the station. Mike shook his head. His thoughts where this story was getting juicy. But he had to do, what he had to do.

He told the men, that he will see them on Monday. He tells them, to have a nice weekend. All Mike could do was to think about the story, he was hearing. Curious about what is to come.

He could not help it, he even brought it up on his date with his girlfriend, Saturday evening. He talked about some of the story he was hearing. She found it to be quite interesting.

The parts of the story, he found to be a little odd. She smiled. When he said where and who, he heard this story from. She sat there and kept her own opinion of that part, to herself. She really liked Mike. So, whatever he was in to, she went along with it. She was more into him, more than a little bit. More than the story he was talking about.

They did have a little conversation on the topic. He goes on to say he was still skeptical, about the story. He did not know if it was made up or was this a real true story.

If it was not true, then chief can tell a hell of a good story. Mia tells him that she has Indian blood in her. He really did not respond to that. He looks at her, then he realizes that it could be possible. Besides, she did have what they called Indian hair. Her complexion could pass as one.

Still, he felt like he was being bias because he was in love with her. So, he could not answer, truthfully. Once she said, she did not think the story, he heard, was that farfetched.

She explains, her grandmother used to tell her, her sisters and cousins' stories about when she was a little girl. Just her grandma did not go into so much detail, like that.

He was always amazed by her intellect, as well as her beauty. When he thought about it, he never thought to ask his own grandmother about this. He always assumed they came from Africa as slaves on a slave ship. Just like he learned in school. He never knew some Indian tribes were enslaved too.

With all, and what he learned in school, had him not knowing what to believe at this point. Still, his girlfriend thought he was a little crazy. She told him that, then kissed him goodnight, after he walked her home.

The weekend went by quickly, besides having a great date with his girl. That night they hung out, kind of late. He knew, he had to get up early for work the next morning. But some things are worth the sacrifice. Young and in love was one of them.

Sunday started off slow at work. By the middle of his shift, the day began to pick up. Before he knew it was time to clock out. Which was good for Mike.

When he reached home, he studied a little bit. He spoke to his girlfriend for an hour or so. He took his shower, then he crashed, he was out like a light. Sleep was needed.

Chapter 15
Town under fire

Monday morning came like the weekend did not exist. Mike gave the men their coffee and rolls. Then Mike and chief got back to business. Mike saw that Chief wanted to share some more of the story. Mike took out his notebook. He reached for his pen.

Mike was ready for Chief to get started. Chief asks Mike, where did he left off at? Mike looked at his last page of notes that he took down. He began to read off some of the last part Chief talked about.

Mike figures, he will do that until Chief could take over from there. Chief appreciated, the fact, the young man really was interested in his story. That reassured him, to tell him some more of it.

Chief began talking about Andrew Parker, Master Parker's only son. His youngest child. Andrew had three sisters older than him. The way Master Parker and his wife was having girls. Most thought he would not have a son to carry-on his family's name.

Then it happened, his wife gave birth to a baby boy. He was so happy everybody on the plantation knew about it. Andy grew up being around slave being on the plantation working for his father.

He inherited some of his father's ways. He also saw things from a different perspective. When the government laid down a road through the parker's plantation. Which left the old slave's quarters on one side of the road. And the Parker's master house, crop fields, barns on the other side. It made the property separate. From the land Andy inherited from his folks.

Eagle and the ex-slaves had to cross the road to work on the Parker's plantation. Andrew got married to his childhood sweetheart. They started a family shortly afterwards. Andy's hires Eagle's wife as his children's caregiver.

After mother chief passed away. April took over raising Andy. All the way until he was a man. He had the upmost respect for her. Eagle still manages the Parker's land, like he always did.

Now, when he goes into town to get the supplies for the old plantation. He also picks up things for his store in his village. In the village they already had houses and school, etc. They added a barber shop and a beauty salon.

Then they opened a church. The village was growing so big, other ex-slaves from all over the south came to live in their community.

Most of them, Eagle knew from childhood. Because they were all united once upon a time as an Indian nation. Way before the invaders came and took it all away. He welcomed different tribes of people with open arms.

In return, it made the brothers of the tribe, Eagle, Falcon, and Buck's rich. The investment Andy made by placing a bank in the village. Turned out to be very profitable.

The Tailor shop Falcon opened gained great success. It was, so good, the white people of the town, went to him for their tailoring needs. He was known as the best tailor in the region. Politicians came to his shop to buy suits and dresses.

Before you knew it, the village became a town, as the population grew. Andrew Parker had plenty of workers to work the plantation. Many residents of the black town were looking for jobs to work. They came across the road by the dozen to the Parker's plantation.

The black town began to be more prosperous than the adjoining white town. Everyone in the area knew it too. As segregation became the heartbeat of America at that time in history. A large amount of white people invested capital in certain businesses in the black town.

As long, as they were making money, one way or another. No one really cared about which of the two town was bigger?

Of course, racist people did not like the fact, but at this point, it was not too much they could do about it. They had no reasons to try to destroy the black town.

Making money in so many different businesses, Andy was the wealthiest man in town. His banks brought in huge profits. Especially in the black town. Andy was the first person to purchase a vehicle in the whole region.

At that time, the average person was still getting around with a horse and a carriage. The Parkers was the talk of the town. The town newspaper which Andy owned, always had something new and innovative for the residents of the town.

For the people of the town, to keep up with the rapidly changing times in the country. America was changing and innovators was leading the way, into the future. When Andy's wife told him, they were expecting? He wanted to celebrate the news.

He decides to go to the bar in town to celebrate with some friends and family. He rounds up his childhood buddies to help him celebrate the good news. He met up with his old friend Ralph at the bar.

His friend Ralph was rumored to be involved with a black woman. Most of the town, did not agree with his choices. He also was known as the town's drunk.

The night before the men met up for drinks. Ralph was sitting at the bar, drinking until he was drunk. Shot after shot of whiskey. He got kicked out the bar from trying to start a bar fight. He Staggered home.

He came home, to incite a violent altercation with the mother of his children. He came inside the house where he finds his wife and children sleeping. He turns on the bedroom light. He asks her why was she looking like a nigger?

He tells her to take the nigger look off her face. Then, he threatens her, by saying if she could not get the look off, then he will. He began to beat her. He was so drunk, you could smell the alcohol through the pores of his skin, through his clothing.

He threatens her again, this time, he tells her if she did not tell him the names of them nigger slaves that murdered Master Parker?

Then he will murder her, right there, that night in the house. He beat her into the corner of the room. All she was able to do, was use her arms and elbows to block some of the vicious hits she was receiving.

From the beating she was getting. She did not know if she will be able to survive much more. He beat her bad that night. She was scared to death. She believed if she did not tell, she will be murdered that night.

The look in his eyes had her convinced. She did not want to die in front of her children. With no other choices for her to make, she had to cave in and tell this man what he wanted to know, so he could stop beating her.

she tells him, that it was Eagle, Falcon, and Buck, who was in the barn that night, Master Parker got murdered. They were the ones who stopped Master Parker from raping her. She does state, that was the last time she saw Master Parker alive.

He got what he needed, to put one and one together. What he got from what she was saying, was the only people that was in the barn that night was, Master Parker, Lilly, Eagle, Falcon and Buck.

Since, they told Lilly to run. Then it was only the tribe brothers who was left in the barn. They must have had killed Master Parker. Because the next morning Master Parker was found dead.

He had all the pieces to this unsolved puzzle. Ralph could not believe that he solved the case of what really happened to Master Parker, the night he got murdered.

Now, the only thing was, how was he going to break the news to one of his closest friends, Andrew. That his most trusted ex-slaves murdered his father. How he found out was by beating his half-white sister, half-way to death in the process, of getting the information out of her.

Not forgetting, his father was trying to rape his own daughter, his sister that his father had with one of the enslaved women on the plantation.

He understood that it would be a lot to tell his friend. He also knew that one day he will have to tell his friend what he discovered.

Still, that was not a good feeling to have, being a true friend of someone, and you know the truth, even though it might hurt your friend. Eventually being a real friend, you have, to let your friend, know the truth.

At the bar that night celebrating Andy's new child, soon to come into this world. The men had so many shots of whiskey and vodka, their skin began to turn red.

Most of Andy's friends was in the Ku Klux Klan. Including his cousin Dave. They felt it was their duty, to uphold and make sure the white race remains superior on American soil.

His friends went on to say, we made the United States, not them. They asked Andy to join a while ago. He did donate to their cause. After it was explained they had preserved what their fathers worked so hard to build and maintained.

Out of fearing of eventually losing everything. Joining the organization was seriously on Andy's mind. To him, his friends was making a lot of sense. After so many shots of whiskey and vodka. Everyone began to talk freely out of their mouths.

At this point, nothing was off limits. Some of their friends started talking about Ralph and his black wife. They called him mentally ill, for doing that. They ask him, how could he have a baby with a nigger. They said, his kids were only part human and part animal. They kept on going until Ralph got mad. He lost it when they called him a nigger lover.

He began to talk about what he had just found out about the murder of Master Parker. He knew how it happened. That caught everyone in the bar attention, especially Andy. He told them, for him to find out this information, he had to beat it out of his black bitch.

The story that changes Andrew Parker's life forever. When he heard the story, he felt betrayed, violated on so many levels. Ralph starts by saying his ½ black wife was in fact, Andy's sister.

He followed by saying, Andy's father, Master Parker was trying to rape his own daughter, that he had with a slave woman, the night he got murdered. He pauses to take another shot of whiskey. He asks Andy did he want him to continue. Dave tells him to continue, he wanted to hear what he had to say about his uncle.

While he was trying to rape Lilly, three tall black slaves came to stop him. somebody asks Ralph, what was their names? Ralph goes on to say, it was Eagle, Falcon and Buck. They saved her, then they told her to run away from the barn. That is when the men stayed in the barn and killed Master Parker.

It was so much for Andy to take in for the moment. His friends were outraged over hearing that some niggers killed Master Parker. Andy anger started with his blood boiling out of his skin.

His friends suggest that somebody must pay for this horrific act of violence. His friend Mark had an idea on how to get some payback. He tells all the men to go home and get their white sheets, they are going to pay them black sons of bitches a visit. Andy's cousin wanted to kill Eagle a long time ago.

That last time they across one another, he almost did. Andy tells them, he does not have a white sheet, now. His cousin tells him to come back to his ranch with him, he has an extra one for him. He instructs, his younger cousin, at this time, it would be best if he did not go home yet.

Andy followed his cousin to his ranch house in the woods, a little away from town. They all met back up in the field as planned. The field was a mutual place that was not that far away from the black town, where Eagle and his brothers lived at. They had on their white sheets. Burning crosses in their hands.

First thing the army of sheeted men did was firebomb the entire, nearly formed black town. One black man who was minding his own business, closing, his store for the evening. His regular activity.

The Militia of men came into the black town, so quickly, the old black businessman did not have a chance to run and hide, to get away. As the hooded men on horses got close enough. One of the men shot the old man on the spot. And kept riding into the town with the rest of the group of masked men.

People began to run to get out of the way of this white militia. They burned everything in their path. And shot whoever stood in their way of completing their mission.

A little black boy witnessed what the hooded sheet men was doing.

He ran all the way to the house where Chief Eagle stayed with his wife and kids at. He warned the Chief that the posse of men were looking for him, to kill him. Eagle knew a day like that one, was going to come sooner or later. He had idea what it was over.

Eagle gathers his brothers, and other tribe's men. He told the women and children to hide out in the back. Where they could not be seen, but they can hide and be safe, out of harm's way.

Chief grabs his rifle and joined his brother and tribe's men, ready to defend their honor. The great war of the two town was on. When the militia arrives at Eagle's house, the land the slave quarters once resided on. Andy then took off his sheet, off his head. His cousin asks him, what was he doing?

He told his cousin, that this was personal. Eagle stood on the side of his house, waiting to attack at any given moment. The men of the tribe stood out of sight of the white men. Andy begins to call out Eagle's name. One of the tribe's men looked out of the side of the house, to get, an, view of where, the posse of men was at? As soon as, he did that, he was shot in the head.

Eagle, his brothers and tribe's men retreated, back inside of Eagle's house. Each man positions their selves at all the windows of Eagle's house. The men got off their horses and positions themselves as well. Some of the hooded men rushes to the back of the house.

That caught Eagle off guard. The men in front began to rush his house. As the men ran up to the front door. The first man, who came through the front door, Eagle shot and killed him. While bullets were flying back and forth of men shooting. Many men were shot, and many men died in the gun battle, on both sides.

One of the hooded men, who were with the group, who rushed through the back, spotted the women and children. The man grabs one of Eagle's children. Which was Eagle's youngest son. He quickly runs to the front of the house with Eagle's son in his arms. The man gives the child to Andy.

Andy calls out Eagle's name. The gun fire ceased. He tells Eagle, if he did not come out, he is going to kill his son. Eagle and his brother came out of the house and surrendered themselves.

The town sheriff intervened. He tells the men dressed in sheets, that these men should be judged in a court of law. If they are found guilty of the charges, they will be executed. The sheriff heard about the allegations Ralph's wife was making against these men. He wanted to make sure she was telling the truth.

The white militia led up, they allowed the sheriff to take Eagle, Falcon and Buck to jail. Later, that night, while Eagle and his brother were in jail. One of the sheeted men returned to Eagle's house. He broke into Eagle's house and raped Eagle's wife, at gunpoint.

He rapes her in front of her children. As she was being raped, he forces her to look at her while he raped from behind. She looks at them as he penetrates her, tears began to fall from her eyes. A memory scar, that Eagle's children will never forget for the rest of their lives.

Chief ends this part with, talking about his grandfather. His grandfather always told him this part of the story with anger, and watery eyes. He tells his grandson, Chief, that he could not get the looked of his mother being rape and violated out of his head.

He always said, he wishes he were bigger and older, to defend his mother, but he was not. That hurt his grandfather's heart, for the rest of his life. Mike was sad at this point of the story.

Pork Chop was not feeling good about where this story was leading to. Chief Pointed out, the day his great-grandmother got raped, that changed a lot of things.

Because by hurting her, you also hurt a whole generation of people in the process. Maybe that was the reason why that man did it, the way he did.

Mike asks about the three brother and Lilly, and what happened to them? Plus, he wanted to know, how did chief know about that part of the story? The Lilly and Ralph part?

He starts off by letting the young man know that Lilly was his great-grandmother's sister. Master Parker raped his great-great grandmother and got her pregnant. Mike was sitting there listening and taking down notes of the story.

But he could not help but feel sad about it all. Chief tells the young man if he wanted to know what happens to Chief Eagle, Falcon and Buck. He will have to wait until the next time, to find out.

Pork Chop reminds Mike that his trains were coming. Chief agrees, neither one of the men wanted Mike to be late for school. Because of missing a train. Mike knew they were right. He boards the train.

While he sat on the train, a lot of thoughts raced through his mind. For one, he was grateful, he lived in the present day. Because the people back then, went through a lifetime of struggles, heartbreaks and pain. Unbearable, to some people including himself.

Chapter 16
Revenge

Chief, the next morning. He got straight, to the point, Mike was prepared to hear some more of the story.

After being raped, that night. Eagle's wife had to think quickly. She knew they will be coming back, for sure. She could not take any chances. She had to make a move. She decides to leave town that night.

She wakes her kids up and tells them to gather as much things as they can carry, in their little potatoes' bags. She went to inform the rest of the people of the tribe, that was left. She explains and tells them the plans of what she was going to do. And they were welcome to join.

She stresses that the white mob will be back, to destroy whatever was not destroyed the first time. She already knew her beloved husband's fate. She knew they were going to put Chief Eagle to death. Him and his brother was already dead, in the eyes of the people.

She had to think about the future. And that was the children. A few of the tribe's men escorted the women and children on wagons through the outskirts of town during the darkness of the night.

They figured, if they move quickly and quietly, they could make it to a couple of towns over by the time the sun rises. They then could board a train to New York City. That was the only choice to be made. Or stay and be sitting ducks, and wait until they decide to kill, them all.

As they traveled on horses and wagons, into the night, to never look back, nor return. When Ralph reached home, he walked into an empty house. With no signs of his wife and kids. They just upped and vanished. He will never see them again.

Lilly knew, she was marked for death. In so many ways, she knew the outcome, would not be in her favor. She had to leave. She felt like, she would die in the process of exposing knowledge of the truth. People cannot always handle the truth.

She had too much to lose to stick around for the outcome. She was right to make that move when she did. Because little to Ralph's knowledge, Andy and the posse of men followed him, home.

They came for his wife. Andy tells him that his wife, Lilly must die. That is the only way, his father's secrets can remain secret. Andy was concerned about protecting his family's name.

If word got out, about his father was having children by slave women, and that he tried to rape one of his children, he had with one of the many slave women, that would tarnish and destroy their family name and credibility. Andy was not about to lose it all, from technicalities.

While he could rid himself of everything by ridding himself of all worries by killing Lilly. They came into Ralph's house. They demanded him to tell them where his wife was at? He told them, he did not know, about his wife's whereabouts. He says, he is looking for her too.

With no hesitation Dave shoots him. Ralph dies on the spot. Dave looks at Andy. He tells his cousin, he did not like nigger lovers, anyways. Andy wanted to know where Lilly was at.

After searching, and searching it was plain to see, she vanished into thin air. While everyone was preoccupied a group of remaining Indians snuck back into the black town that was burning.

The building that housed the Parker's bank was burned down and wide open. It was easy access to the money that was inside of the bank. The men stuffed money into large bags.

They jumped back on their horses. They wanted to make one more stop, Buck wanted to go to the Parker's plantation, for the last time. He set the Parker's crops on fire. Then he got back on his horse and him and the men who accompanied him, rode towards where the women and children were headed.

That same night, after the men went to pay Ralph a visit. They all went back to Dave's ranch. After drinking some more shots of whiskey and vodka. Andy was talking to his cousin about the only thing he wanted to know from Eagle was, why?

Why did Eagle murder his father? While taking some more shot of whiskey. Andy states, he wanted to know why? Then after that, he is going to kill Eagle, for his father's death. Andy went on to talk about the sheriff.

He felt like, the only person standing in the way of him killing Eagle, was the sheriff. Dave reminded his younger cousin, that they were in the south. The south deals with things the southern way. Andy wonders what can they do?

Dave's friend who works as a sheriff's deputy, told Andy there is a way to get Eagle tonight, if that is really what he wanted to do?

They knew that is what they wanted to do, they wanted to see if Andy was willing to take it to another level. After Andy agrees, he wanted to kill Eagle that night.

The sheriff's deputy pulls out the keys to the sheriff's office, and jail cell keys from his front pocket. He knew exactly where Eagle, Falcon and Buc was being held at.

While sitting the jail cell, they noticed that they must have mistaken Buc, for another one of their tribe's men. They planned not to say anything either about the mix up. They were happy, that at least, their brother got away.

The posse of men went into the town. They reached the jail cells where Eagle and his brothers were being held at. They took the men out of the cell at gunpoint. They tied the men up and placed them in a wagon, and transported them back to the black town, where Eagle and his brothers built and lived at.

They wanted to show the black community who was really in charge. Whose country this was. They first beat the men, then they tied them to three trees. They place ropes around their necks.

Chief Eagle was a very tall man. Andy Parker was a short stubby man. When he talks to Eagle, he must look up towards the sky. Dave was average height for a tall man. Even he had to look up to see Eagle's face.

Eagle, Falcon and who they thought was Buc, were positioned to be hung. They did not waste time in hanging Falcon and who they assumed was Buc.

Andy prolonged the hanging of Eagle. He needed to know why? He did not care if they had to stay out there, all night long, to get his question answer.

Then that is what he was prepared to do. When he asked the question, he did not have to wait so long for a response. Eagle tells him the truth. Eagle talks about how they invaded his peaceful world. And took it for their own.

Master Parker was horrible to his people of his tribe. He states that Andy's father enslaved his people. And if he had the chance to do it all over again, he would do so. Andy got so angry from the last words Eagle said.

He pulls his knife out and stabs Eagle in the heart. Blood begins to gush onto the ground. Andy states that this is for his father, he stabs him a couple of more times.

Eagle look towards the skies. It begins to rain. Andy signals his cousin. Dave pulls the rope to hang Chief Eagle. What made the men scared, was the fact, Chief Eagle smiled while he died a most painful death.

The blood that exited the body of Eagle and his brother ran out of their bodies onto the ground and ran through the town, like a river.

Andy, Dave and the posse of men left. Eagle, Falcon and the tribe's man who was mistaken for Buc, hung from a tree by rope in the heart of the once prosperous black town in America.

A black town that was ahead of its time, turned into a thing of the past. Easily forgotten history, that will be buried, in history. A story that would not be taught to the masses.

The next morning, the sheriff goes in the sheriff's office station. He checks the jail cells. He wanted to wake the prisoners up. He realizes the men were not there when he reached their cells. The sheriff tells his deputy to stay at the station while he checks out what happened to the prisoners.

The deputy stood against the wall on the side of the entrance of the sheriff's office, he smiles because he knew what happened to the men the sheriff was looking for.

The sheriff jumps on his horse to go find out where were these men at? He thought, Eagle and his brothers escaped. He knew where to find them, he only had one place in mind, he could think of. He rides his horse into the black town. He sees everything was destroyed, abandoned, and burned to the ground.

He views dead bodies all over the town. He notes later in his life, that the black town looked like a war was fought inside of it. He could not believe what he was seeing with his own eyes.

Then he looked up because the sun was in his eyes. Plus, sweat was forming on his forehead. He takes out his handkerchief to wipe his forehead.

That is when he saw Chief Eagle, Falcon and another unidentified man hanging from the tree, life-less. It was so dark the night before, nobody was not really paying anything, any attention.

The sheriff noticed that one of the three guys was not Buc. He arrested the wrong guy the night before. He knew it was plain to see. The sheriff could not help but notice, Eagle was dead with a smile on his face. The feelings he felt, after what he saw brought chills up and down his spine.

It was a very haunting feeling. After that, he quickly got back on his horse and rode out of town. He needed to know what happened the night before.

He starts his investigation with the now known suspect, Andy Parker. He rides to the Parker's Plantation. He wanted to question Andrew about his whereabouts, the night of the murders of Robert and James Greenland. And an unidentified man.

He reaches Andy, he tells him, that someone took Eagle, Falcon and another man out of the jail and hung them in the black town, the night before.

The sheriff tells Andy that one of the brothers got away. Whoever killed Eagle and Falcon, did not kill Buc. The sheriff wanted to see Andy's facial expression and his response about the new information.

Andy answered the Sheriff, as he looked at the floor. Andy was nervous about Buc, still being alive. Now, he had to worry about one of them coming back for him. But he held his own with the sheriff. He reminds the sheriff that his father elected him as sheriff of their town. The sheriff was not moved by that statement.

Andy lets the sheriff know. He did not have anything to do with it. He did mention that he was glad someone did. Because he honestly told the sheriff, if they did not do it, then he would of did it, if he had the chance. He said it in a privileged manner.

He keeps saying inappropriate things to the sheriff. He reminds the sheriff that these men murdered his father. The sheriff reminds him, they have laws to deal with these things. And at no time it is all right to take someone else's life in retaliation.

The sheriff explains that Robert and James Greenland got murdered last night. He tells Andy to think about that. He tells Andy that he will be back, to talk to him a little bit more about the situation further.

Andy walks back inside his house. Where he did think about it. After the sheriff leaves the property, Andy came back outside. He looks across the crop fields, straight beyond to the other side of the road. The town that once was. Now, it was destroyed and burned down to the ground.

He wondered why he was able to see, so far from his porch steps. He looks across again to see if anybody was still there.

He heard what the sheriff said, Buc is still alive and out there. He looked to the ground and when he saw his own crops were burned to the ground, he realizes he took a noticeably big lost. He checked again, out of paranoia, there were no one there, the old black town, now resembles a ghost town.

Andrew decides to ride into the black town to investigate for himself. He took his gun with him, just in case if he sees, Buc or if he sees Lilly. He wanted to clean up whatever mess he done made. He stopped in the old burned down black town.

He stops at his bank, which was burned down as well. He did notice the safes of the bank were opened. Also, besides the money that got burned up in the fire. A substantial amount of money was missing. He was not worried about that for the moment.

He rode on to Eagle's house. He arrived at the spot that once was Eagle house, it too was burned to the ground. And his family was gone too.

That is when it hit him, yes, he got his revenge on his father's death. But he lost everything in the process. A little later in time, the sheriff did come back, and he had enough evidence to charge Andrew Parker with the deaths of Robert and James Greenland.

Dave warns Andy to keep his mouth shut about who was involved with him, the night Eagle and his brother got hung. In fact, he suggests that Andy says nothing at all. He tells his cousin that no white jury will convict a white man for killing a black man, in the South.

Andy was arrested and went to trial over the charges of killing James and Robert Greenland. At the trial, the prosecutor gave a great case. He was able to place Andy at the scene of the crime. But he lacked true evidence because of evidence tampering.

When he turns it over to the judge? The judge in return turns the case over to the all-white jury. Just like his cousin said, Andy was acquitted of all charges. He left the court building a free man.

Afterwards, with all the publicity he received from the trial and all. The people of the town lost respect for him. Even the Klan wanted no dealings with him anymore. They felt Andy was too close to be telling the truth. They could not have anyone like that, around their organization. Andy's wife wanted a divorce from him. Their relationship was never the same.

Feeling ostracized Andrew felt the best thing to do was to leave town. He liquidated his assets. Then he left town for good. Rumor has it, he went out west to start a new life. With him leaving with all his money. The little town could not sustain a loss of money of that magnitude.

So, the town went bankrupted. Just like the black town, the white town was to be lost in history, as well.

After chief finishes up telling this part of the story. Pork Chop was looking at the floor with tears in his eyes. Even Mike, who was trying so hard to hold back the tears. Had watery eyes. Because this part of the story was so deep in its own.

Pork Chop asked about the people who left? Chief looks at his friend, he tells him after his grandfather watched his own mother being raped, in front of his face.

Of course, no one could possibly be normal after witnessing such a disrespectful activity. Chief tells Mike, that there still more to the story, he wanted to tell him.

Mike takes his eyes away from staring at the floor, to look up, and answer Chief. Mike said, ok to that.

Mike was happy his train came that day. Because on that note, there was not anything left to say. That was deep beyond deep.

Chapter 17
Harlem

They arrived in Harlem, in New York safe and sounded. A little under a decade before the great Harlem renaissance era. During this time, many southerners migrated to the cities across the country.

They blended in with the others. Everyone left the south to find better lives in the city. Harlem was a place that was huge for black people in America at the time.

Eagle's wife and children reunited with Eagle's sister Spirit and others who left prior too. Spirit plans a huge Sunday evening dinner for everyone after church.

Eagle's wife and kids met up with Eagle and his wife's eldest daughter Malwee. Malwee and Spirit asked about Chief Eagle and Falcon?

She tells them what happened. She explains, Eagle, Falcon and the town they built was all gone but not forgotten. She spoke with tears running down her eyes, onto her beautiful high cheek bones. She did not leave out any details, she tells the story in its entirety.

As they were listening to the story being told, everyone who were listening began to sob too. They talked about it in the kitchen before they brought out the dishes of food they had prepared for Sunday's supper.

While they were placing the dishes on the dining room table. Spirit told April that she always knew her older brother was going to kill the person or persons who had any involvement with taking away our freedom and our land, that our ancestors live on for thousands of years.

Lord knows, they tried, but they could not take away our culture. Spirit felt her father taught them that. She knew it was all just a matter of time. She remembers how her brother felt when they were children watching their grandfather being killed in front them by the invaders.

The bitterness Eagle carried inside himself. It got to the point, it consumed him. As he grew older, the hatred grew inside of him. She states with everything that happened, he had every right to feel, the way he felt. Those people stole his world and replaced it with their own.

She felt bad about her brother's fate. Both her brothers, Chief Eagle and Falcon. She felt no remorse for Master Parker at all. She despised Master Parker in the worst way. For all she cares, he could rot in hell. Spirit never forgot when Master Parker raped her. Spirit was shocked when she saw her only remaining brother Buc.

Buc explains further in detail, on what had happened from a perspective, who was there, to witness how it went down. When the sheriff grabbed the wrong person, who he thought was him. He just went with it. Buc was aware, if he did not do that, he would be facing a guaranteed death.

It was so dark, and they were so racist. They thought all black people look the same. That was a prime example of that. Buc remembers when they saved Lily from getting raped by Master Parker.

Once they saw Master Parker drag Lily into the barn, they knew he was going to rape that little girl. That is when they made their move. It was the perfect time to do so. After they stop him from raping her.

The rage and adrenaline kicked in, and they murdered the old master, in cold blood. April, chief's wife bring to all their attention, was the fact, that Lily was her younger sister. From the results of Master Parker raping her mother.

Buc began to put one and one together. He could not believe Master Parker was trying to rape his own daughter. He knew Master Parker was a sick disgusting man. But this was another level of a sick being.

Everyone at the dining room table shook their head, about it all. Before he left, he mentions, him and some tribe's men burned the Parker's plantation fully. They knew, that left a permanent scar on the plantation's business forever. That put a smile on his face, for the moment.

Still, he was a little sad, he could not celebrate this moment with his brothers, Eagle and Falcon. He understood sacrifices was necessary, to get their tribe, to where they are at, now. Chief's grandfather, young Eagle, who was still a child at the time, ate with his cousin at the children's table.

His grandfather was 9 years old at the time. Spirit notices the room full of people was looking sad and low-spirited. She reassures everyone that everything will be all right.

Also, to never forget their family's history and build on the tribe's legacy. Our future starts now, we navigate the outcome. She says to everyone in the room, we must live long, and free lives dedicated to the ones who sacrifice their lives for us to get this opportunity to live.

Eagle's wife, April was never the same. She lived a private, distant and lonely life. She was hurt, distraught, sadden, and traumatized over the things, she is experienced and endured. She was not mentally stable anymore. Everyone knew it too. But she still tried and tried again to live without thinking of the past. Which was an impossible task.

They were able to locate the whereabouts of April's sister Lily. She was living in the state of Illinois, not too far away from Chicago. April and Lily reunited a couple of times. When they met up, she tells her sister her part of the story.

The reason why she told on Eagle, Falcon and Buc, was because she was beaten by her husband at the time, Ralph. She thought, she was going to die that night. She had no choice. April told her; it is okay.

The main thing was you did not die. She did not fault her for what she did. She understood, she had to do what she had to do. Lily explains to her sister, that she knew once the Parkers found out about everything. They would take her life before the truth could came out, about Master Parker being her father. It was such a secret. Master Parker forgot he raped their mother. And that is how she was conceived.

That night in the barn, he looked into her eye, and treated her like a stranger to him.

That was sickening to them because their mother always said she had eyes like her father. With her choices of men, she dealt with. The relationship with the sisters grew sour. Lily still loved her white men. She remarried another man from the North. They had a couple of kids besides the ones she had with Ralph.

There is nothing wrong with her choices. It was her right to do so. The sisters did make plans to see each other periodically. Time was not kind to them. April passed away at the young age of 38.

Some said, she died of a broken heart. The doctor said it was a heart attack. What got most people was, she was not even 40 yet. The family was saddened by this great lost.

Especially, Charles, that was little Eagle's named given at birth. Young Eagle was raised by his aunt Spirit, his uncle Buc, and his older sister. He was 15 when his mother passed away. His uncle Buc taught young Eagle the ways of the ancestors. The tribal lifestyle.

Unfortunately, at this point of time, they were far away from the tribal life. They were living, in a big city now, country life was all but irrelevant.

Still, they were able to still past down their rich history. The next decade ushered in great times in Harlem.

Harlem was the place to be for black people in America. So much culture, unity, and all-around love on the streets of Harlem at the time. It was not just a neighborhood, it was community. Charles went to school, and he learned a lot on the streets of Harlem. Family history was taught daily, his uncle said, that one day he will have to pass the knowledge of the family, to generations to come.

He fell in love with Harlem. He used to tell his grandson later in life, Chief, it was so much to do in Harlem for a black person. He never thought so many black people can own so many businesses. It was completely the opposite of the south he knew.

He even talked about having an inside the house bathrooms. All of this was new to him. He knew his mother and father taught him a lot, even though both their lives were cut short.

As he grew into a man, he cherishes the times, he had with them both. During his high school years, he worked at his aunt's laundry/ cleaners, shop. That is where he meets his future wife.

Chief emphases on that part. Because that is when his grandfather met his grandmother. First, they were great co-workers. Then they became great friends. Which lead into love. All the way to a wonderful relationship. From there to a great marriage. When they got married young Chief was 20 years old.

He became Chief Eagle, like the ancestry linage states, when they gave birth to their first child a baby boy. Chief's father was born. A new young Chief.

On another sad note, Chief tells the young man, he did not know his father that well. All he knew was the experiences, he experienced being around his father. Because time was limited with his father?

His father was murdered when he was 6 years old. Something that no one ever brought up. He got most of his knowledge he has from his grandfather. His grandfather did say to him that his father died a chief.

As far as, the family's tradition ritual states, when chief was a child, he was called young Eagle by his grandfather. And his grandfather was called old Chief. Every summer, up until the passing of his grandfather when he was 15 years old.

Before that, for years him and his little sister would take the greyhound bus to upstate New York and spend the whole summer at their grandfather's house.

By that time, his mother moved them to Brooklyn. Even his mother knew, some of the tribe history on his father's side of the family. His mother always said, her family was Indian too. The natives of another tribe, in another part of the south.

She made sure we knew that many Native Indian tribe were reclassified to being African. So, by law, they would not have any rights to their land. She always praised and adored his grandfather for teaching us, their Indian history.

His grandfather made sure they knew their family history. He spoke about the family's stories so much, him and his sister knew these stories by heart. He taught them, knowing the history by memory, was the way the ancestors documented history of the tribe.

Written documents came with the invaders. Just like stealing land and creating a whole bunch of laws of the land in favor of the oppressors. His grandfather always says, nobody could tell you, your history better than your own family.

The greatest words of wisdom his grandfather taught him was knowing your family linage and history is the greatest treasure one can have in one's life. He held on to that message deeply in his heart.

After the passing of his grandfather. Chief honestly stated his whole demeanor changed. He admits that he was a disgraceful young man to his heritage and to himself.

The only things he did good in his life was he graduated from high school. He met a great woman and had two daughters. He joined the army and served a tour in Vietnam.

During the Vietnam war he got hook on to the drugs. Heroin was the drug he got addicted to. He came home not the same. He did finish his tour in the army, in Vietnam. He became a dishonorable veteran. Due to his excessive drug use.

He committed petty crimes, to feed his drug appetites. With his drug habits, he loses contact with his children's mother and his kids. When he got convicted of a crime he did not do. The last time he saw his daughters, his oldest daughter was around 7 years old. His youngest was 5.

With no money to get a private lawyer. He had a legal aid, with his arrest record, he was sentenced to 30 years in prison. His children's mother visited a couple of times.

But after a while and him being shipped further away upstate New York, he lost contact with them completely.

Bad choices and a bunch of non-smart moves got him into predicaments that he has been dealing with to this current day. He faults only himself.

Mike listened to the elderly man as he spoke. The message the old man taught hit the young man's soul. Chief thanked the young man for giving him a time of a day.

Mike was happy and honored to hear such a great story of a man's life and history. Pork Chop was speechless. He was completely touched by the amazing story his fellow army veteran and homeless friend told.

He jokingly tells Chief that he has been around him for all these years and he never heard this story before? Pork Chop also mentions that his family is from the state of Illinois. He was born in a little town, not far away from Chicago.

He also tells them, that he too had Indian blood in him. Pork Chop tells him, his great grand grandmother was Indian. He heard that from his grandmother. Chief looks at his friend. Mike looks as well. Mike was about to laugh at Pork Chop for making the statement.

Until Chief says, he could see that. He goes on to say to Pork Chop, just a small percentage though, an exceedingly small percentage.

After Chief shows just how small by the fingers on his hand. They all laughed about that. Then Mike looks at his watch. The train was coming, he tells the men that he must go.

He tells, the men he will never forget this time. He made sure, he told Chief that he is going to copy his notes that he gave him. So, chief will have his own copy of the notes he gave him. Chief liked that a lot.

Chapter 18
Maturity

Mike re-wrote the notes of the story. He made a neat copy for himself and a copy to give to Chief. He places his notes into a safe place.

He places the notes in a plastic crate where he kept all his personal documents and important papers at. He moved the crate with his other things when he moved out of his grandmother's apartment in the projects. He moved because he wanted more space and privacy.

He rented a room, in the same neighborhood his grandmother lived in. Just a couple of street blocks away. As his relationship got more serious with his girlfriend, he knew he needed even more privacy.

His mother was released from prison a couple of weeks later. His mother received her degree while she was in prison. She also became drugfree. When he saw her, he noticed she gained a couple of pounds. She looked exceptionally good.

He saw a smile on her face, which he did not see in an awfully long time. His mother also was part of a program in jail that provided housing. She got an apartment, and his sisters went back living with her. Mike felt good about that.

His mother came home in time, to go to Mike's college graduation. She was able to be there. And that meant everything to her. That was a special day for all of them. After he completed a two-year community college. He was offered another scholarship to continue his education in the city's university.

He rented the room for a short period of time. Mainly due to the fact, his roommates were on different paths in life, than he was. It was not because he felt better than the next person. He just outgrew the confinements of what was around him.

Nothing more, nothing less. He grew tired of his roommates' antics. The loud music, at all times of the night. The apartment always smelled like weed. The alcohol use brought out multiple personalities in certain individuals. That led to fights and the police presence in the apartment he lived in, constantly.

Mike was trying to study to reach his goal. He did not need the distractions. He went to the platform in search of Chief to give him a copy of the notes, as promised. He looked through-out the platform, he did not see any signs of either of the homeless men.

He got on the arriving train in the station. He went to his new college further in the city. Afterwards he went to work. He still worked at the local supermarket. He got promoted to the assistant manager. A job that earned him some more, mostly needed money.

After a couple of days of looking, searching for Chief and Pork Chop, he realizes, he probably will not see these individuals ever again. With all the things that was going on in the apartment his was renting a room in. He decides to get an apartment with his girlfriend.

He moved a few blocks away. They got engaged shortly afterwards. He first, sat her down to explain his life, the past of his father abandoning the family. His mother's struggles with drug abuse. His older brother being incarcerated.

The way he feels, now. And what is his goals and ambitions in his future. He wanted her to know everything before they take extra steps into the future being together.

He sat and listened to her past, present and future goals, also. He really loves his soon to be wife. He wanted everything to be pure and organic.

She reassures him, she was in love with him too. That made him feel good inside. He knew, at that point, he was not alone anymore. And that is what he needed in his quest of living a healthy and grounded life.

Chapter 19
Evolvement

Mike began his new life in Queens, New York. Time began to speed. It took little of no time for him to get his second degree. He graduated from the city's University with a B.A. in journalism. He married his long-time girlfriend, college sweetheart.

Then he went on to graduate school and got his master's degree in English. He started his teaching career as an assistance teacher in the New York city public school system. He taught different grades in English.

He wanted to explore one of his hobbies, which was writing. He began to get serious about writing a book. He wrote a manuscript. He submitted his manuscript to several publishing houses.

After waiting a couple of months, a company accepts his manuscript. They liked his writing style and the way he put a story together. He receives a book deal from a publishing house.

His first book did all right. It did enough to get him a bigger book deal. He landed a 5-book deal from a prestigious publishing house. He got the books contract when he hired a book agent. He signs his contract for an undisclosed amount of money.

His first couple of books he wrote under his new contract, did well in the bookstores. His books created a buzz. But not enough for him to quit his day job.

He and his wife went on to have 4 children. 2 daughters and 2 sons. With both of his salaries and his wife's salary they were able to live an extremely comfortable and solid life.

Everything was going well until he had hit a roadblock, more like writer's block. He could not create an idea worthy enough to write a whole book about. No vision to say the least.

While his brain was on freeze. The book deadline was vastly approaching. With the burden of losing his book contract. He knew, he had to fulfill his obligations. He had to think quick on his feet.

Looking through his crate trying to find old notes that he wrote in the past. He could not find nothing that caught his attention. He pulls out a crate that was more deeply buried in his garage.

He looks to see what was in this crate. He did not check inside the crate in years. He pulls out one of his folding chairs to have a seat. He sat down and dug into the crate.

He was seeing things he has not seen in over 15 years or so. He stumbles across some old notes. The story, he wrote the notes for the old homeless man he met in the train station. Who he came across, while he was in college? The story the old man told him about 15 years ago.

After going over, it with his wife. She was not sure where he was going with his thoughts about the project he wanted to do. Even if she was not sure about what he was thinking about doing. She was going to support him in anything, he wanted to do.

Even though she was a little skeptical about it. He read his notes, and just like when the story was being told to him by Chief. He was so intrigued by the story line.

After thinking more about it. He decided to use the notes. He composes the notes into book form. He reviews it a couple of times.

Then he submitted the manuscript to the publishing house. He did not know what to expect the outcome would be. Or, how the publishing house will perceive this book submission.

He knew, he was gambling with a chance. A chance he was willing to take. He could not help, but to be nervous about it all. This book was different, in contrast compared to all his other books, he authored prior to.

The story was not the problem. One thing he did while he was in college, even though his major was English literature. His minor was American history.

Mainly, Black American history. That is when he discovered a lot of what the old homeless man was saying was, true. His accounts were fully accurate with his story. There were not many doubts in his mind about the story.

He just did not know how people will respond or react to the story. All authors feel like that when a new book of theirs comes out. That was normal for a book writer.

After a couple of weeks of not knowing, his agent calls him. He tells him, the publishing house loved his submission. They wanted to release the book as soon as possible.

His publishing house representative wanted to get the book on shelves at the bookstores. The editor told him it was a great book.

She told him it was a new insight, on what transpired in the past in American history. She asked Mike, how would, he classified his book? She was sure, he was going to say non-fiction.

She was shocked when he told her it was fiction. He tells her it was not a true story. The editor told him it felt like a real story to her.

Mike states, the story was based on a true story to many. But he did not have any physical evidence. He could not prove if the homeless man were lying or telling the truth. There were some accounts that was true.

It was not enough for him to classify the new book as a non-fiction book. He never saw the old homeless man again. Ever since he left the neighborhood years ago.

Chapter 20
Prepared

Mike woke up in the morning to the sounds of his children playing in the room next to him. Also, the aroma of breakfast being cooked in the kitchen. His alarm clock goes off. To get an extra minute or two of sleep. Mike hit the snooze button a couple of times.

His wife walks into the bedroom, she asks him if he was finally going to get up? She kisses him. He touches her behind. They both smile at each other. She tells him, they have a noticeably big day ahead of them. She smiles, she lets him know, they could finish what they were doing later, when they get home. He did his chuckle at the fact.

He tells her to come closer to him. She knows exactly what is on his mind. And what he wanted to do. She explains to him, she is not falling for that trick on this day. She reminds him of the importance of the day was.

For some weird reason, Mike was extra laid back about the day. And what it meant to him. Even though this day was the most important day, so far as an author, in his life.

After a decade or so, of writing numerous books. The book of notes he was not ever going to use ends up being the book that will define his career as an author.

That was hard for him to understand. A book of notes he collected back in his college days. From a notebook that was packed away deep in his garage in a plastic crate, that had dust on it.

Turns out to be a smash hit in the book industry. The book sales soar through the roof. They could not keep this book on the bookstore shelves. His book was in high demand. Everyone wanted a copy of it.

In return Mike receive the biggest royalty check, payday of his life. He became a very wealthy man from being on the best seller's list for a couple of months.

With all the money he receives, he was able to afford to buy the big house on the hill, that he promised his mother, one day he was going to buy for her.

He tried to get out the bed, but he decided to lay a little longer. His thoughts were his wife always wanting to be early for every event. She wants to be prepared hours before.

He figures, he still had enough time to take a nap. That did not happen the way he planned it. He officially got up with his human alarm clock, his baby girl. His daughter jumps on the bed. She grabs a pillow from the bed.

She throws it at her brother. Mike opens his eyes when he felt the wind of the pillow being thrown. His eyes were opened wide, just in time to catch his son, ready to throw the pillow back at his little sister.

By this time, she was hiding behind Mike, on the bed. He knew it was time to get up out of the bed, for good. He asks his younger kids about the whereabouts of his older children. His daughter, who love telling everyone's business to him.

She tells him, her sister got up in the morning, took her shower, then she got into her car and drove off. She looks into her father's eye, she says, she asked her could she go with her. Her sister ignored her. When she wanted to know where she was going? Still, she got no answers.

Mike looks at his daughter with a puzzled look on his face. He did not know what to do or say about any of the things his daughter was talking about. He did get the information, he wanted from her.

He asks his young son about his brother. Before his son could answer the question that was being asked. His daughter cut her brother off.

This time she at least kept it simple and plain. That is the way Mike liked it. She tells her father her brother was outside sitting on the porch. And he has been out there all morning.

By this time both of his younger children were sitting on his bed complaining about being hungry. The rules of the house were everyone eats breakfast together. The house cook knew not to serve anyone breakfast without the authorization from him or his wife.

He calls the kitchen to tell Maria it will be all right to serve the little one's breakfast. He was not even mad at the kids. Waiting on his teenage children, for them to be ready. They will be waiting there all day, for them to come to the dining room.

Mike strolls into the bathroom. He places his shaving cream on his face. He gathers all his necessities to get into the shower, shortly. He shaves off all the unwanted whiskers off his face. He wipes his face with his hand towel. He brushes his teeth. Then he undressed to get into the shower.

Afterwards, he walks into his walk-in closet, with his towel wrapped around his body.

He looks through his suits collection, to see which suit he was going to pick to wear for the special occasion. His wife walks into the bedroom. She notices, he was in his closet. She walks into his closet. Mike places the suit he chose, on the rack in the front.

While he was matching a dress shirt, a tie and socks. She waits to see what he will pick out. Once she saw what he chose. She suggests he should wear his tuxedo to the award dinner. He agrees. He again, tries to get fresh with her.

She tells him to stop that, as she smiles looking into his face. She tells him her make-up was done. She did not want to mess up her make-up.

He went back to searching for his tuxedo suit, she helped by looking for his tuxedo shirt and find a bowtie to match her outfit for the night. She wanted them to be color coordinated.

He asked her, where was Junior? He tells her, he did not see him all morning. She tells him the same as his younger daughter told him, he was outside sitting on the porch alone. She suggests he go and talk to their son.

After Mike got half-way dressed. Meaning, when he put on his pants and tank-top, and his shoes. He went outside to the porch, where his son was sitting in the corner bench. He sat on the bench next to his son. He asked his son what was wrong?

He noticed his son was sitting there, with his head hung down, looking depressed. His son talks about a paper project that he had to do for school. Mike wanted to know what the project was about. His son spoke about the school project that he had to do.

But he had no clue whatsoever, on how to approach it. Mike felt what his son was saying, could be an easy solution, so he thought? His son breakdowns the school project, for the most part he had to talk about his own family history.

Mike knew he had to probably sit down with his son on this school project. Mike knew that the only thing, he knew about the family history. He is willing to share with his son, which was not a whole lot.

Due to the time and pre-engagements, he could not do the project with his son that day. He really did not know what time him and his wife would reach home after the award ceremony.

He plans with his son to do the project the following day. Before, he walks away from his son, he lets him know that he loves him. His son smiles and tells him that he loves him too.

He went back inside the house to finish getting prepared for the evening events. He walks back into his bedroom. He checks his cell phone on his nightstand. He browses through his phone, checking different social media apps.

He presses the icon that stated he had a missed phone call. He then noticed he had a new voice message. So, he checked the voice message first. He listens to the voice message of his mother telling him to call her when he got this message.

The big house on the hill, he brought for his mother. Technically, it was for his mother and grandmother to live in and share. One of his little sisters stays there with her three kids. That is another story. The problem with that all was the broke, unemployed guy she was dealing with, also lived there too.

The thought, on how he was going to deal with that, was on the back burner of his brain for the moment.

Besides, he did not who was worst, because his other little sister always borrowing money from everyone in the family, to support her, her kids and her broke baby father. Mike chooses to pay that sister's rent because he did not want that train wreck anywhere near his mother and grandmother.

When he reached his mother on the phone, his mom wanted to know, what time should she and her mother be ready to come downstairs to be picked up by the car. She asked him, would he be able to accompany her and his grandmother to a funeral later in the week.

She lets him know it was for her mother. And it was especially important that they support her on this one. He tells his mother what time the car will be arriving to pick them up. Also, he states it would be an honor to escort his grandmother to his grandmother's friend funeral. He tells her, he will see them shortly. He ended the call on that note.

He sent his daughter a text to locate her whereabouts. She texted him back, saying she went to get her nails done and have breakfast with her girlfriends.

He did not even question it. He knew and understood teenagers are going to be teenagers, especially teenage girls.

Chapter 21
Accolades

The same evening Mike receives the Pulitzer Prize award in fiction for his book. He goes onto the stage to accept his award. He knew from the award committee, he had to keep his acceptance speech short. He went up to the podium and kept his acceptance speech short but sweet.

Mike first thanked God. Then he thanked his wife, mother and grandmother. Last, but not least, he thanked Chief. The crowd erupted in applauses celebrating his accomplishment.

He took a newspaper photo with all the other award recipients of that night. He was introduced to a lot of people. He shook a lot of people's hands. People who were the upper echelon of the entertainment industries. The important people of the world.

He and his wife had an amazing time at the event. His mother and grandmother spotted quite a few celebrities. They took some pictures with some of their favorite celebrities. Many people from many famous walks of life, were there to cheer him on.

It turned out to be such a proud moment and milestone in Mike's life. Only a limited number of Authors can say they won a Pulitzer Prize in their lifetime.

The significant of the award he received reached its peak, when the celebrities he saw, asked him would it be all right, if they could take a picture with him?

Talk about a surreal moment for him. The crazy part was the same people if he would had saw them not even a month ago. He would have asked them for their autograph. And if possibly get a photo with them.

So many people in the crowd were taking picture of them with their cell phones. It was impossible to know who had pictures of him and his wife. He went from a nobody to somebody in a heartbeat. He first came across the fortune. And now the fame.

Still, he could not comprehend the feeling he had of being incomplete. He felt like something was missing. He did not know what or who, was missing. It was a gut feeling, he had inside. He was feeling like he got fame and fortune off writing someone else's story.

His initial feeling was yes, he was happy. Yes, he deserves all the accolades that came with it. He smiled that night to save face in front of the crowds of people who were cheering him on.

Behind the smile was another story. That he only knew. His life changed that night. While having dinner at an upscaled 5-star restaurant in the city, where he took his wife, mother and grandmother to.

When the waiter came to the table with the bill. The waiter tells him, the owner said the meal they had was on the house.

Then a bottle of champagne on ice got rolled over to the table Mike and his family was at. The owner of the restaurant walks up to the table to greet Mike and Mike's family. The restaurant owner wanted to congratulate Mike, himself personally for winning a Pulitzer Prize.

Then he invited everyone, to help him give a toast to Mike Greenland. His wife, mother and grandmother placed their glasses of champagne to toast Mike with the restaurant owner. Mike's wife, mother and grandmother embellishes in the generosity of that was shown. Mike thanked the restaurant owner. The last thing the restaurant owner wanted from Mike was he wanted to take a picture with him. after that they shook hands.

Mike appreciated and enjoyed every moment of it. He never felt this way before in his life.

While he waited out in the front of the restaurant for his driver to pull up with the town car. When his driver arrived, he told the valet parking attendant to go and get his wife, his mother and grandmother. After the young man brought the women out, he opens the town car door.

Mike pulls, the young man to the side. He asked the young man did he know who he was? The young man smiles, and says yes, you are the man who was on the T.V., who won the writing award. What the young man said, had Mike stuck for the moment.

He really did not know the award ceremony was televised. He was not expecting nor prepared for the instant fame. He knew winning this award was big. But not as big as it got. This was a first-time experience for him. He tips the young valet attendant with a twenty-dollar bill. The young man thanked him.

The young man asked Mike could he get a picture with him on his phone camera. He tells Mike, he wants to show it to his mother. Mike liked the young man's attitude. He allows the young man to take the picture.

He gets into the town car. His driver drives off. First, they drop off his mother and grandmother home.

In the car, on the way home, his wife carried on how proud she was of his accomplishment. She states winning a Pulitzer award is a huge milestone in a writer's life. She was well, aware of what it meant, to achieve that pinnacle. She was an educator too. As being a teacher herself, she was overwhelmed with joy and happiness for her husband. She tells him, she has a treat for him, when they get home. Mike smiles and kisses her.

They got home shortly afterwards. Most of the kids were in bed. Well at least half was. The younger ones. His oldest daughter walks up to him. She gives her cell phone to her mother. She asks her mother to take a picture of her and her daddy.

Something she has never said before. That had both her parents shocked. She barely wanted to be seen with her father, less than a week ago. Like all teenagers. Now, he was her best friend. They knew something was up. He did not ask why she wanted to take a picture with him. He just took the picture.

Mike really did not care about the reason why? He will take a picture with his daughter anytime. Even though he and his wife knew their daughter had some type of motive behind it.

She tells him, that her father is famous. And she feels like everyone should know it. Plus, she went on to say, everyone needs to know, she was his daughter.

After her mother took the pictures, she gives her phone back. She kisses him on the cheek. She states, he is the best dad in the world. Then they looked at one another. She tells him, she going to use his favorite line, so he does not have to say it to her.

She acknowledges that she was putting too much sauce on the chicken. All three of them laughed at that one. She knew, she was overdoing it. That was his favorite line, when he felt like someone is overselling, overdoing it, to persuade to get their way.

She was serious about the pictures she just took with her dad. She made sure she had a picture with her dad holding the Pulitzer's prize. She immediately posts the pictures of her and her dad online to show her friends on social media.

To her, the celebration was on. She finally felt like her father was cool. For the moment. Thoughts of a teenager. She figures, she will milk this as long, as she could.

Mike made his way to Junior's room. He opens his bedroom door. He sees Junior playing his video game in the dark. When he asks his son was everything okay? Junior raises his hand up to signal everything was fine. Mike thought maybe Junior might had saw something pertaining to him winning the award. Maybe he would of saw him on T.V.?

Then he thought about who he was talking about. He realizes his son was probably on that video game the whole time, they were gone. He knew, his son did not know what was going on in the real world, besides the video game, he was playing. Teenagers are weird in their own way, right? But as being a parent of teenagers, you get used to weird.

The following morning Junior goes outside to get the newspaper from the lawn. He takes the newspaper out of the plastic bag. He unfolds the newspaper. He noticed his father's picture on the front page. He could not believe what he was seeing.

He runs back into the house. He shows everyone except Mike. Mike did not wake up, yet.

Mike wakes up as usual, after hitting the snooze button several times. Then he finally gets up, out of the bed. He stops in the bathroom to do his normal routines.

When he reached the kitchen. Everyone was already sitting at the kitchen table. He notices everyone was quiet and smiling. He did not know what that was about?

So, he asked the only person in the room, he knew would spill the beans. He calls his youngest child to him, his baby girl. He tries to whisper in her ear, to see what was going on. She begins to laugh when his lips touch her little ear. He does it again, same results. This time everyone heard what he was asking her?

Finally, Junior walks up to his father, opens the already folded newspaper. He then, points at the picture of his father on the front page of the newspaper. Mike takes the newspaper away from his son. He glances at the photo of him on the cover page.

He then turns to the page of the newspaper, that the cover page says the article about him was on. He locates and reads the article for himself.

In the article, they compared him to the likes of Alex Hailey, Toni Morrison and a bunch of other great Authors of the past. He was incredibly grateful, humble and honored just to be mentioned in the same breath as these great Authors.

He still felt incomplete, the feelings of, feeling like he did not accomplish his accomplishments by himself. He does acknowledge the fact, he used Chief's story for, the majority, of his book. He just added the part of a young college kid meeting two homeless men on the train platform.

While he served the homeless men hot buttered rolls and coffee. During, him serving breakfast to the men. One of the homeless men decided to tell him his story. About himself and his family history.

He ponders about when the old man told him to chart down his story, and that is what he did. The old men predicted this story will be a great book for the masses to know about. The public did receive the book in great numbers. Mike wrote all the notes down as instructed.

Also, he injected the actual story of meeting these great men. Even though the men were labeled as street bums. He knew, he takes the credit of putting it all in book form.

With all of that, he still felt like maybe he owes somebody for the success he is receiving. The more famous, honored, and praised, the more he felt like he owed, or at least, share with the person who gave him the story.

Not just because the book made him rich and famous. It also saved and rejuvenated his written career. Mike knew that for sure. He knew, he was never that creative to come up with a story like the one the old man gave him.

For now, he wanted to sit back and enjoy the fruits of his labor. Everything that took place was surreal to him. A moment beyond his wildest dreams. He could not think this would had been the outcome.

A moment like this only comes once in a lifetime. He reflects on where he came from, to where he was at. At the present, moment.

That is what made him grounded and humble to recognized and realize, blessing when he saw them. He deserves all that has been given unto him.

Chapter 22
Chief

Later in the week he prepares to go to the funeral with his mother and grandmother, as promised. He only questioned, going to a funeral for a person he did not know. He thought that was a little odd.

That is what he told his sisters when he spoke to them about it. His sisters told him that grandma told them to be there. So, that is where they will be at. He could not help but to think he is going to a funeral of a complete, stranger.

He knew, his grandmother did not want him to come because of his new fame and fortune. If he thought like that, then he must be crazy.

He gets in touch with his mother. He thought maybe she had some more information pertaining to the funeral. She was completely honest with him. She did not have a clue. She says she is going to support her mother, no matter what. He went off the momentum his mother provided.

He finishes up getting prepared for the event. His wife was ready a long time ago. She was waiting on him. Until he got ready. That is when she decided an outfit change.

His driver drives up to the front of the house with the town car. He asks Mike, do he want him to go to the back and take out the Escalade, since it was going to be a nice amount people going with them.

Mike agrees with the suggestion. While his driver went to the garage to get a bigger vehicle. Mike goes back inside to see if his younger kids were ready. He sees them sitting on the couch fully dressed and ready to go. He tells them to go to the bathroom. He did not want to make any pit stops.

His wife comes downstairs looking elegant and beautiful as usual. They all walked out the house and got into the vehicle. The next stop was to pick up his mother and grandmother.

Once they arrived at his mother's house, everybody who was going was packed into 3 to 4 cars. His mother and grandmother got into his vehicle.

Then they drove off with the other vehicles' following behind. Mike was the type of person who needs to know what he is getting himself into.

While they were riding in the truck in route to the funeral. Curiosity got the best of him. To the point, he could not take it anymore.

The suspense of not knowing was killing him. He goes on to ask his grandmother about whose funeral was they going to? She politely turns her head and ignores the question, he asked her.

He then looks at his mother. Then his mother asks her the same question, he just asked her. His grandmother's response to the question had everyone shocked in the vehicle.

When she said, she was going to the funeral of her children's father. Everyone in the car got extremely quiet. His grandmother states, since everyone wanted to know, so bad! Then she says, so there, now you have it.

His grandmother turns her head to continue to look out the car window. Mike's mother was speechless. She was at a loss of words. Mike had a question for the answer he just heard.

He then asked his grandmother how many kids did she have? It did not stop there. He asked her how many baby fathers did she have? As Mike carried-on asking inappropriate question to his little old grandmother. Mike's wife sat beside him looking at the floor of the car. Embarrassed to look up. She knew, he took it way too far.

All she could do is shake her head in disbelief over what was being said. Mike's mother became completely offended with the questions Mike was asking her mother.

But she also wanted to hear what her mother has to say about that? His grandmother was not really in the mood to answer a bunch of stupid questions, now.

She was mourning the loss of someone who she loved dearly. The father of her most precious gifts, her children. Instead of answering the nonsense questions, she did one better.

She tells everyone in the car, if they did not want to go to the funeral, then they do not have to. She wanted them to drop her off at the church and leave. And she will find her own way home.

Mike's smart mouth youngest son says ok to what grandma said. Then looks at his father's facial expression. Which was blink. His then went on to say, she said we could drop her off, and we could leave.

Mike looked at his mother. Everybody in the car did. Then Mike looks at his son, this time his son could read his father's facial expression and it was bad news for him. He tells his son he did not want to hear another word from his mouth for the rest of the day. Nobody did not say anything for the rest of the ride.

They all realized that grandma was focus and determined to do what she set out to do. When they arrived at the destination.

Everyone gets out of the car behind grandma. Nobody was going to leave grandma by herself. Everyone exited the car except Mike's mom.

You could tell she was nervous over the whole ordeal. She tells Mike, she did not want to go. She even suggested that they go ahead with grandma. While she will wait for them in the car. She felt like, she did not even know her mother anymore. She has known this woman, her whole life.

The one thing her mother never did was keep secrets from her. So, she thought. She wonders why she would keep this secret from her. The main problem was Mike's mother was his grandmother's oldest child.

Now with all that was being said. She was not sure about that anymore. She knew, the last time she saw her dad, she was only 7 years old.

After that occasionally, she would ask her mother about her father. After about x number of years of asking. Her mother told her.

Her father had passed away. Now she sat there in the car, confused about it all. Mike sees his mother is serious about not getting out of the car.

Mike walks up to his grandma. First, he apologizes for the way he was acting inside the car. He knew the only person who can make sense out of all this would be his grandmother.

The only person that could get his mother out of the car would be her own mother. His grandmother pushes her walker back to the car. She sits on her walker's seat part. His mother opens the car door.

His grandmother starts off, by saying she was only trying to protect her from heartbreaks. She admits she was heartbroken, and it did not make any sense for her children to be heartbroken too. She tells her, her father kept on going in and out of prison.

With his drug use, and abuse. She knew then, he was not ready for a family. So, it all was a matter of time, he chose drugs and the street life over having a family. Which she refuses to allow her and her children to go through that. She had to look out for her children. That was most important to her.

Once upon a time she does acknowledges her kid's father was a tall, handsome, intelligent man. who has she loved dearly? He was an all-around great man. He just got caught up in the lifestyle.

She explains to Mike's mom, when his mom got hook on drugs and had to go to prison, that broke her heart. She says, she saw signs of him through her. After having two daughters with this man.

He finally tells her to leave him. When he knew, he was facing a lot of prison time. He wanted her to know, he did not commit the crimes, the charges state he did. He did say, he did not do it.

Not having a lot of money and being black in that period, of time in history. His criminal record of going in and out of jail. He knew the judge was going to throw the book at him. He told her to leave him, because he did not want her to throw her life away waiting on him. While his life rot away in these prisons he will be staying in.

That was the last time, she saw him. It was about 60 years ago. When she went to prison to pay him a visit. That is when he said what he had to say to her. He stresses the fact she could do better without him.

She tells Mike's mother that was around the time she was about 7 years old. When her mother said that. Mike's mother was able to put one and one together.

Even though, Mike's mother does not remember her father's face clearly, anymore. It was about 60 years ago. When she thought about it, she did remember seeing her father in a jail suit. Also, the fact, that he could not leave with them.

She remembers, she was not allowed to touch him. That was the last time she saw her daddy. Just like then, a tear, followed by many tears covering her high cheek bones. The story her mother told her, brought her back to when she was a little 7-year-old girl, seeing her daddy for the last time.

It hurt her then and it hurts her now. Protecting your children from heartbreaks, she could relate to that all so well. Even though she chose to indulge in her baby father's activities, and it screwed up her life in the process.

Which took an exceedingly long time for her to get her life back to normal. She understood where her mother was coming from. She gets out of the car, to everyone's delight. She hugs and kisses her mother.

She thanks her mother for being there for her, no matter what she has gotten herself into in her life. She assists her mother up from the walker seat. Then she tells her mother that she loves her.

Mike stood there with the rest of the family standing next to the churches outside steps. Mike asks his mother, what she wanted to do?

She smiles at her son. She holds her mother's hand. She tells him, she is going to her daddy's funeral. Mike grabs his grandmother's other hand. He looks at his son, and the rest of the family members who were in attendance. He informs them all, he was going to his grandfather's funeral.

Mike's son carries grandma's walker up the church stair. While Mike and his mother hold onto grandma to provide support, while grandma walks up the church steps. Everyone else followed behind.

They walked inside the church as a family, like they were, strong and together. Unified by lineage. They sat in the middle of the church sanctuary.

Until the sister of the deceased saw Mike's grandmother. She knew, who her brother's children mother was.

Also, her brother has two daughters. The last time she saw his daughters was so long ago. But she could tell by their features, who they were. They looked different, but similar. Their family genes are strong. To the point you cannot deny the family presence in their appearances.

She asked the usher to change their seats. She wanted them to be closer to the body. The usher explains what they wanted to do to Mike's grandmother.

His grandmother got up and moved to the front row. His mother and Aunt sat on the front bench with their mother. Everyone else filled in the rows behind them. Mike's daughter went to sit with her grandmother, in the front row in the church.

The view of the body from where they were sitting at now, was so close. You could almost see inside the casket. Only a side face view of the deceased man.

Mike saw a recognizable face. He could not put his finger on it. But he automatically, felt like he saw this person face before. He did not know where?

He whispers to his wife. He tells her, he knew the person in the casket.

He was told to hush and be quiet. He was not trying to disturb what was going on. He understood why they told him to be quiet. So, that was what he did. He did not stop staring at the deceased man in the casket.

Trying to figure out who this man was? And where he knew this face from? His grandmother sat in between her daughters. As the funeral service went on with occasionally his grandmother shedding a tear or two. Reminiscing about the good times, she spent with the love of her life.

The love they once had was so strong and wonderful. It produced two lovely, smart and beautiful daughters. Mike's aunt had no recollection of her father, at all. She was only 3 years old, when her father went away. His mother and aunt could not help but to be nervous. And sad at the same time.

After, the kind words from family and friends were said. After, a couple songs from the choir and a few soloists sung songs. Encouraging words from the Pastor of the church.

The moment had arrived. The moment everyone anticipated came. The viewing of the body of the deceased.

His grandmother went first. She gives him a kiss. Then she says farewell my love, under her breath. She walks back to her seat. She cried a little. She takes a piece of tissue out the box of tissue the usher provided. She wipes the tears from her eyes.

His aunt went up next. She stared at her father that she never spoke to. Who couldn't she recall ever meeting him? So many different emotions ran through her thoughts. As she looks at this man she has never known.

Mike's mother walks up to the casket to hold her sister's hand. Mike's mother realizes that at least she knew their daddy for several years. And she did not know too much. She could only imagine what her sister was feeling. Her sister only knew their father for three years. And that was at the beginning of her sister's life.

She was more concern about her little sister than herself, now. Her sister's son and daughter came up to the casket to get their mother. She walks back to her seat, wanting to see her father's face, at least one more time. She needed more time. This was the first time she ever saw her father. Her kids sat with her as she cried.

Mike's mother had her back to the casket watching to see if her sister was all right. To her mother, she was procrastinating the inevitable. When it came time to view her father's body. Mike's mother looks back again. She looks at her mother. Her mother points at the casket.

Then she had to do, what she had to do. She watched the life-less body of her creator. Even though, he was not there to create a lifetime of memories. They still felt compassion for the man who helped to create them. Mike's mother walks away with tears running down her face.

After seeing that Mike already had a tear in his eyes. Mike's wife and kids were next in line to view the body. They glanced at the body and kept walking by. Her daughter had tears in her eyes when she saw her grandmother crying. She was emotional like that.

Mike's sisters followed, afterwards. They stopped and looked at the body. And they too, kept walking. The tears came when they saw their mother and auntie crying.

Mike's walks up to the casket next. Nervousness already was kicking in from seeing his whole family crying over a man in a casket that most of them never met.

Still, he wanted to see what all these emotions were about. He looks, into the casket. He takes a deep look into the deceased man's face. He began to place a hat on this man. And a beard with some dirt.

Then it popped into his head, who this man was? He realized he was looking at Chief. The homeless man, he has been searching for. To find completion to his thoughts. The person who he wanted to compensate for the story that was given.

The man's story of his family's history changed his life, forever. Then it dawned on him? The story he was told and wrote about, was in fact, his own family history.

Mike was beyond shocked about it. That day turned into a bittersweet, priceless moment. Just like Chief had once told him, he learned his family history from his grandfather.

Now, Mike stood with tears in his eyes. Relating to the feeling. Now, he could say proudly, his grandfather taught him, his family history.

What an amazing thing to experience. Such an indirect gift. Mike had to thank the universe for all that had transpired.

Too him, it was like his grandfather was telling his family history to a stranger. So, he thinks? Or was it a universal connection that made Chief compelled to share his story, to this, young man?

On a funny note, he could not believe how clean and sharp Chief looked in a suit and tie. Mike stood up there viewing the body so long, his wife had to get him to escort him back to his seat.

He cried for many different reasons. With all pertaining to Chief. Nobody else knew, why? Only Chief and Mike understood why? If he would had known, that was his mother's father, he would had surely told her, he was in contact with him.

After the funeral, he told his grandmother about the book and Chief's connection to it. The fact, the storyline was based on a story Chief told him. She looks and smiles. She says the only man she knew named chief was the father of her children.

She noticed the story did seem, to be extremely familiar. When she read it. She recalls, Chief telling her the story of his family, when she got pregnant with Mike's mother.

She mentions, it was about 67 years ago. Chief wanted her to teach their daughters about their family history. The history of their culture.

His grandmother explains, she got caught up in the life and times. She worried more about raising her two daughters as a single mother during these drastically changing times in America.

She admits, she forgot to do what she promised Chief, she would do. Mike started to notice how his grandmother was feeling as she talked about the past.

Mike tells his grandmother not to worry about it. The last thing he wanted to do, was to get grandma upset. That was not his intentions. The one person he did not want to upset was his only grandparent he has ever known, who was vital to his upbringing.

Who made him the man, he is to this day? Most credit goes to his grandmother. His grandmother suggested that fate brought the two of them to cross paths. She went on to say, for Chief to pick him, out of all the people in the world. He must have seen or felt something about him. she did ask where did he meet Chief at?

She asked Mike, was Chief one of the homeless men that he provided with coffee and buttered rolls. Mike says, something like that. Then he quickly changed the subject.

The family decided to go out to dinner on the way home from the funeral. His grandmother agreed. Only if they were going to celebrate Chief's life. Not to dwell on the negative parts of it.

Mike really does not talk about the fact, that Chief was homeless at the time. No one did not know about that, maybe only his wife, if she remembered. Everyone agreed with grandma. To celebrate Chief's life.

Mike's mother was fascinated over the book Mike wrote. She liked before. Now, after knowing the true story of the book. She went from liking to loving the book. The book was based on her family's history and on top of that, one of her sons got time to spend with her father. That was priceless to her.

To have a book about her father and their ancestry. She could not ask for much more. The whole family was happy, celebrating and enjoying each other in conversations. Mike was almost complete.

He felt he had some unfinished business to take care of. He reflects on when his mother, younger sisters and he were living in the shelter, homeless. His mother's drug abuse got them kicked out of the shelter. Him and his sisters had nowhere to go.

Luckily, he was wise enough to call his grandmother. He went on thinking about how an act of kindness impacted his life in so many, different ways and levels.

Chapter 23

Inheritance

Mike had some free time on the weekend. He woke up early Saturday morning. He woke up before anyone else in the house did. He goes to his home office. He turns on his computer. He gets on the internet. He goes to check on his books sales. His book was still on the top seller's book list.

After checking a couple of other things. Including his e-mails. He decides to do a background check on Chief. Since, now he knew Chief's government name. Which was Thomas Greenland. The same last name they shared, that he did not know about at the time. When they met face to face on the train platform years way back.

He had already promised his mother, he would do that. They wanted to find out more about her father. Yes, Chief told him the story and history of the family. But he did not talk much about himself to him.

What Mike discovered after doing a background check on Chief. Was that Chief had inherited some acres of land from his great grandfather, Chief Eagle.

Mike goes into the bedroom to wake up his wife, to tell her about what he had just found out. She wakes up out of her sleep, with her eyes still closed.

He just needed to tell her. He needed to tell somebody. Someone had to know about what he discovered.

Then he left the room to go back to his home office. His wife went back to sleep.

At least she tried. She gets up to use the bathroom. She stops in Mike's office to speak to him about what he had just mentioned to her.

She tells him, she always believed that things happen for a reason. When you do things out the kindness of your heart. You will be blessed in life for your services.

She remembers, when Mike use to tell her about taking cups of coffee and buttered rolls to give two homeless men in the subway. She tells Mike the universe has favor in him and his family. She told him to keep her informed with his findings.

Then she leaves the office and goes back to bed. He did not understand what she meant by that statement. He went along with what she was saying because he did not want to start any problems in the household. Mike with his inner-thoughts, and mental jokes.

Weird enough, he knew exactly what his wife was talking about.

He decides to call one of his college buddies from back in the day. His buddy who became a lawyer. He had some questions, he needed answers to. He knew his friend would be best qualified to answer, what he needed to know.

He wanted to know was his findings pertaining to owed land, legit or not? His friend told him he will get back in touch with him within a couple of days. And as expected his friend gave him a call a couple of days later, just like clockwork.

He tells Mike, there were land his grandfather inherited from his great-grandfather. That was still in his name. Mike was pleased with the information he was receiving from his long-time friend.

One thing, his lawyer friend did state, was the property belonged to the next of kin. Also, it is public documents that states this. Mike understood that chief's daughters was next to kin. Which was his mother and his aunt.

He understood that. It just meant the land belongs to his mother and aunt now. And he was cool with that. He thanked his friend for the information he found out for him.

He acknowledges the fact that he greatly appreciated the help. Mike got the information he needed, to get started.

Mike gives his mother a call to let her know what he has found out. He spoke to her for a while about his findings. He talks about the land she and her sister inherited, that was in her family's name for generations.

His mother was ecstatic to hear the good news. She tells Mike, she could not wait to share the news with her sister. She knew, her little sister needed something to cheer her up. Especially, after seeing her father for the first time at his funeral.

After she spoke to her sister. Word got around the family quickly, about the land they own now. His mother calls back Mike a couple of hours later. She had so many questions on behalf of everyone she spoke to, pertaining to the land.

She starts off by telling him, she really did not know what to do with some land. She barely knew what that meant? She explains, she did not have a clue, on what to do next? Mike suggested to his mother, was first they needed to review the land to see what they were working with.

She agrees with the suggestion. Mike and his mother planned a trip to go down south. They wanted to get a look at the land for themselves.

Mike's aides his mother through the whole process. And all the necessary paperwork to legally own the land again by law. They stayed in the little town down south a few days.

Mike had to e-mail a bunch of papers with particularly important information on them. He needed his lawyer to check over. He wanted to make sure everything was right and legal, before his mother and him sign any court documents.

When that part was finished. He and his mom drove to the location to view the land. To see what they owned now. It was a bunch of bushes and trees. You could not hardly see anything, at first.

They could not see, any signs of someone ever building anything on the land. As they travel more inside the property on a single dirt road. Mike stopped the car and they got outside of the car to walk around a little bit.

Mike and his mother felt the warmth of the rich soil beneath their feet. It was so much life within the land. The flower was fully blossomed.

The trees looked full and beautiful. They walked around for a little while. They got back into the car and followed another dirt road that was adjoined to the initial one. The dirt road led down to a river.

They got back out the car to get a view of the river. The water looked pure, and the water of the river ran for miles and miles, as far as the eye can see. A breath-taking view. They liked what they were seeing.

They got back into the car. They followed all the necessary dirt roads. Which led back to the major road. To get back to the hotel they were staying at. Mike knew they had to move before it got too dark outside. Because if they did not? It would had been a difficult task, to see through the darkness, of the country night.

On the plane back to New York. They knew it was an exceptionally large piece of land they owned. Both did not know what to do with such a huge land mass like that.

His mother tells him, she never owned anything of that magnitude before in her life.

His mother asked him for his opinion. He tells his mom he might have an idea. But nothing solid yet.

Chapter 24
Humanitarians

Mike's barber came to the house to give him and his sons a haircut like he always does, every two weeks. Mike and his older son were waiting while his younger son get his haircut.

Junior reminds Mike about his school project. He explains to his father, his history paper was due Monday morning in school. Mike remembered. Even though, it probably seemed like he had put it off. Not because he wanted to.

It was due to the fact of Mike being busy with things relating to his book. The award show and things of that nature. Not to mention all the things that has taken place. He was not trying to make excuses. Some of the things that was going on, was life changing events in one way or another.

He told, his son, they could work on his paper after they go to the mall. After, they get their haircuts. Junior liked the plan. Junior sat in the barber's chair.

Mike's youngest son takes a seat next to him. His younger son wanted to know what were they going to the mall for? His son tells him, he needs a new pair of sneakers. He also, said his mother told him, he needed a new pair. Mike smiles because that was the reason why they were going to the mall in the first place. His younger son was excited about that.

Due to the fact, he knew his wife took their daughters out in about. Which consisted of getting their hair done, nails done and a whole lot of shopping. After him and his son got their haircut.

Since his wife and daughters made it a mother and daughters' day. Why not have a father and sons' day at the mall.

Mike pulls into the mall parking lot. He parks his car. He sees a homeless man at the door that led into the mall. Mike and his sons walk pass the man. While they were walking by, the homeless man asked them if they could spare some change?

He went on to say, anything would do, because he was hungry. He needed something to eat. Mike younger son reached into his pockets and gave the man a dollar.

Mike knew his son gave the man all that he had in his pockets. Mike loved the fact his son was willing to give his last to help benefit someone less fortunate. That meant a lot to Mike.

Plus, he liked the fact, he did not have to make his son feel compassionate about helping others. Mike was about to make Junior give twenty dollars to the homeless man.

Mike thought about it, instead of offering him some money. He offered the man to come with them. Mike wanted to buy him something to eat. The bum turned down the offer.

Before Mike could say anything else, Junior reaches in his pockets and gave the homeless man five dollars. Junior questions his father's moves.

He did not understand why his father would want to walk into the mall with a street bum. He did not see the logic in that.

Mike explains more into detail, he knew the homeless man was hungry and he wanted/ needed something to eat. Mike understood, the homeless man was embarrassed to walk into the mall.

Figuring people would judge him, and stare at him. Why would he want to go through the hassle? People who go through many things in their life. To get into the predicaments, they are at in the present, moment.

Mike talks to his sons as they walk in the mall. Mike comes up with an idea, as he always did. He tells his sons to stay where they are at.

He had to go back to the car to get something. He was just making up a reason to go back to the mall parking lot. He really wanted to go back to speak to the homeless man. He came back up to the man, he asks him what size sneaker he wore?

The homeless man thought Mike was crazy, for asking him that. But he gave his foot size anyway. Mike tells the man. He will see him when he leaves the mall. Mike met back up with his sons.

They continue to walk through the mall. Mike came up with an awesome idea. While they were in the sneaker store getting sneakers for all of them. Including the homeless man in the mall's parking lot.

Mike bought a pair of sneakers for the homeless man that was not too expensive. Because he did not want the homeless man to get rob for the sneaker by someone in the street. And he did not want him to sale the sneakers either.

They finished shopping. They stopped at the mall food court. They ate and Mike ordered an extra order to go. His plans were to give the food to the homeless man.

During their time in the mall, they picked up a couple of things in the mall. Including some clothes as well as footwear.

Right at that moment, he came up with an idea of what they can do with the land, his mother had inherited. They arrived, back in the mall parking lot. They saw the homeless man standing by the door.

Mike sends his oldest son to give the homeless man the bag, with the sneakers in it. Then Mike instructed his younger son to give the man the bag with the food inside. The man thanks the young men. He waves and smiles at Mike. Mike waves back.

His sons' saw the homeless man's face lights up, because of his smile. It became one of them things that was a learning lesson. Being taught on the spur of the moment. Without saying too much, in the process.

Helping people makes the soul feel good. You cannot help but to feel proud about that. When they reached home later in the afternoon, Mike tells Junior to get his bookbag and meet him in his home office. Which was technically the basement in the house.

Since, he was waiting for Junior to come downstairs. Mike sat and reflected on the times when he was on the train platform classified as homeless himself.

Helping homeless men with some food, that he barely had himself. That is when one of the homeless men said to him, that he has a story to tell.

Helping the less fortunate gave him, strength, life not only in a story. But a grandfather he did not knew existed. He could have easily missed out, on all that transpired in his life on some many different levels.

If he had chosen to ignore and look down on these homeless men. Where would he had been at in life? if he had done that? What if he did not think to help people that was hungry? There would had been no opportunities.

He felt lucky. That he made the right decision, to care. Over self-thinking. Only thinking about himself.

Juniors came down to the office with his bookbag. He takes out his laptop, he places on his father's conference table. The place where Mike would normally have his meetings at. Junior clicked on to his file, where he had his paper, he was working on.

Now, Mike and Junior were ready to get started. Mike wanted to know what information his son came up with, so far? Junior starts off with saying, they came from Africa. And they were slaves. Then they had grandma, etc.

Before he could get any further. Mike interrupts his son. He tells him to delete all the stuff, he already had on file.

He asked his son because he had to know. Who told him, what he wrote down? His son admits, he was having problems with this paper.

So, he asked one of his classmates to help him out. He got a little information from her. Also, he seeks out the help from his teacher. Both, of them basically said the same thing, that we came to America as slaves on a slave boat. Junior just went off the suggestions, that were given.

Mike already knew, what that was about. Living in an upscale community. Where not too many black people lived at. With only a hand full of kids, of color in the high school Junior went to. Mike knew what to expect. So, he just tells his son, do not let anyone tell you, your history. Because they will always tell and teach false information pertaining to the false indoctrinating narratives that built America.

Plus, he tells his son, that nobody could tell you, your family history, like your own family can. Mike paused for a second. He remembered when Chief told him the same thing.

Junior was trying to comprehend what his dad was saying, but he could not. He did not have a clue. Mike goes to his book shelve. He takes out the book he authored, about his family history, that he newly found out about.

Junior sat there confused with what his father was doing. Junior stressed the importance on how this class was. He tells his father, if he does not pass this class, he will not be able to graduate in a couple of months.

In a nutshell, he tells his dad this paper will be a major part of his overall grade. Mike looks at his son, as his son runs off with the mouth. He could tell his son was extremely nervous over this class.

It was good to see his son was completely committed to this class and this class paper. Mike states to Junior, that this book he handed to him, has his family history inside of it. The family history he learned from his grandfather. Junior did not attend the funeral.

That made Junior out of the loop, to properly understand. He tells his son to use the book as a guide to do his family history on. He instructs Junior to work on his term paper.

After he finishes his paper. Mike said he wanted to read it. If necessary, they can over it a couple times more before Monday morning. Junior did what his father told him to do.

Chapter 25
Building

After he was done with helping his son, with his son's term paper about their family history. Mike gives his mother a call. He wanted to talk to her about a vision he had about what to do with the land his mother inherited.

When he tells her his idea? She tells him, his idea would be perfect. His idea embodies everything that has to do with humanity.

Mike got in contact with all his friends, who knew about different aspects pertaining to his idea. Things like building permits, construction permits. All the legal aspects of the business part of his vision.

He met up with an architect to come up with different ideas on how the buildings will look like. when it is finished. He has his first meeting with his family to explain his vision for the newfound land they now owned.

After his family lecture, he shows them several model ideas on how the buildings will look like. Also, he showed the actual blueprints to all several model buildings, to the ones who understood how to read them.

Afterwards, he gathers everyone in the family together. He wanted to take a vote with the show of hands, on what building designs they liked best for the buildings?

The building that suited them best on what they were trying to do. Within, a couple of months from the family meeting. Construction began on the Chief Eagle living Center for adults. And the building next door would be called the Chief Eagle senior living center.

During that same summer Mike's older brother gets released from prison. While his brother was incarcerated, they told him about everything that was going on.

Now, he was able to take part in the family plans, they had in store. His brother loved the vision Mike had for the family. His brother read his book in prison. He read it a second time, when they found out the new information.

Knowing the story was really about their family history. While in prison, his brother did some research of his own. What he found out was the book his brother wrote about their ancestry, was true in many ways.

The book gave him hope in jail. He just knew, it was something bigger out there for their family.

He acknowledges the fact of not only did Mike got an opportunity to meet their grandfather, but he also was able to obtain their family rich history.

A history that nobody even knew existed. Mike was a type of person to never step on anyone's toes. So, when he told his older brother technically, they should call his brother Chief. Mike remembers what his older brother did and was trying to do.

In many cases his brother did sacrificed his life and freedom to protect his mother, his sisters and even himself for all hurt, harm and danger. Even putting food on the table at such an early age.

Being there for him and their little sister when both of their parents were chasing the drugs.

In all due respect his brother deserves to be called Chief. Mike's brother was humble, happy and proud about being called Chief.

But he tells Mike, the only way he will accept being called Chief was if Mike be called Eagle. If so, then he will be fine being called Chief. Mike's brother was about sharing with his little brother, he always was like that since they were kids.

He felt Mike did it all. All the footwork to get the family to this point. Mike was the one who met their grandfather.

He felt like it would only be right. Mike liked the way his brother broke it all down from his perspective on this matter. Mike only wanted to acknowledge the fact, in their family tradition, it states his brother would be the new Chief of the tribe, which meant family in this case.

Mike's wife was pleased with what her husband was doing. The whole family knew at the time, the main reason why Mike came up with the idea was from Chief and Pork Chop.

After he explained the story to them. Which by then, they all knew Chief was either, their father, grandfather, or great grandfather. It made sense to everyone who was in attendance for the second family meeting. Everyone was on board.

The second meeting did bring a bigger crowd than the first. Mike's brother was more of a hands-on type of guy. He decided to be more hands-on with the construction part of the process. He learned a lot about construction while he was in prison.

Mike's part of the project was to find funding for the project. At this point he was mostly paying out of his own pocket.

Mike began his journey to look for the right people to invest into the building fund.

While in the process of doing this his lawyer friend gives him a call. He asked Mike did he know anything about a lawsuit for wrongful imprisonment by his grandfather.

Mike told him, he never heard anything about that. He made sure, he let his lawyer know he was interested in finding out, about all the information that was possible. He talks about his findings in detail to Mike.

He started off informing Mike that his grandfather was incarcerated for 35 years. He served all that time in prison for a crime, he did not commit. He went on to tell Mike, the city had come up with a large settlement amount.

That settlement happened 20 years ago. And nobody has claimed the lawsuit money. A settlement that was never collected. Money which was owed to him and his family.

His lawyer broke it down in simpler terms. Simple, there was money Mike's family could claim from his grandfather's lawsuit settlement.

His lawyer wanted to know what Mike wanted him to do with that information.

He came with an option. He could file a notion in court on behalf of the estate. Mike told him, he had to inform his mother about it, first. Before he could make any decisions about it. He tells his lawyer to obtain and prepare all the necessary paperwork to start the process.

Mike knew, he needed all the money he could get for the building project. The building project was becoming awfully expensive, more than he projected it would be. Also, Mike did not want to go broke funding this building project.

Mike calls his mother. He explains the wrongful imprisonment lawsuit her father had won against the city of New York. Plus, his conviction was overturned. His mother got extremely quiet on the opposite line of the phone. Tears began to run down her pretty face.

One of the things she kept inside herself for all those years was the resentment, the hate, she had towards her father. Mainly, because he left her, her little sister and her mother.

And now to find out, he was in prison all of them years over something he did not do. It all began to make sense when he finally was released from prison. He did not have anybody or anywhere to go.

He did not even know how or where to look for his family at. She could not imagine how it felt to be lost in this world. She felt bad for what had happened to her daddy. She could tell, her father had a very rough life. It was not any doubt about that.

She instructs Mike to do what he got to do to get what was rightfully owed to her daddy. Mike called his lawyer back to proceed with the filing process.

Mike's mother walked into the bedroom next to hers' where her mother stayed. She wanted to tell her mother about what she just heard. She sat down with her and broke down all the new-found information about her father.

Her mother began to cry with her. Her mother says her dad always said, he was innocent of all the charges that was against him.

Due to the way the justice system was back in the day, when it came down to a black man's innocence or guilt. The system always leans towards guilt. Plus, the fact he did not have much money at the time to fight the case. He knew it was going to be a battle for his freedom. When you are a black man in the justice system, you are first guilty.

And then you must prove your innocence. Not innocent until proven guilty. All Mike's grandmother could say was, oh my God, she could not believe how much Chief went through with all of that.

Just facing the fact, the justice system was not made for everyone. It was not made to have justice for all. Mike's grandmother and mother hugged and cried. That was all they could do at the present time and moment.

Chapter 26
Pay Back

The family came to an agreement with what to do with the settlement of the lawsuit money. Which consisted of enough money for the whole family can live comfortably.

Since, Mike was already living well-off without the settlement money. His book was still selling well. Most of the money Mike received from the settlement. He just invested it into the building fund.

His brother and sisters and the rest of the family donated a nice portion of their money into the fund as well. They came up with enough money to complete building the building. And with some government assistance.

The Chief Eagle living Center for adults. And the Chief Eagle nursing home for Seniors. Opened that winter. The whole family was in attendance for the ceremony. Mike's mother and aunt cut the ribbon to officially open the living centers.

Afterwards, Mike held a big family meeting in the conference room in the Senior Living Center. He informs everyone in the family. They have stock in the company that runs the living centers.

Someone asked him, what did all of what he was saying meant? He explains it simpler for those who did not understand. He breaks down the logistics. He let all of them know, they will be receiving a check every month for being a shareholder. Everyone in the conference room was happy to hear about that.

On the site where the two big centers were located had a great deal of undeveloped land. The family decides to build a housing complex, which consisted of a dozen town houses. Almost like a gated community of their own.

They decided to name the housing complex Greenland. Which was the last name they were given. The housed community was built with each house having a huge backyard leading to the big river.

The living centers had huge grounds for activities, along with huge backyards. Inside the facilities were great big dining rooms and day rooms for the residents. A huge recreational center.

A place where people who did not have anywhere else to go. A place where the elderly could spend their later years at.

A place to house some people who otherwise will be homeless. Somewhere for all these people could live and have a good life.

Most of the family decided to stay for a while. Some made plans to move into the houses when the construction was done. Which was theirs to do whatever they please.

Mike's brother tells him, that he was staying. His brother stresses to him, he did not have anything in New York to go back to.

Since he was about to have his own house. And he was barely making it in the city. He might as well stay there with his soon to be wife and soon to be child's mother. Mike agreed and understood where his brother was coming from.

Mike's brother offered to keep the buildings clean. Mike tells his brother he did not have to work for anybody anymore. Knowing his older brother's pride, they agreed he could be the supervisor of the maintenance operations on the grounds of the entire inside and outside of both living centers.

Both, of them knew he just wanted to work a job. Mike understood that.

Mike tells his brother they could go more into detail about what his brother would be doing with his new title and position. when he gets back from New York City.

Mike had to go back home to take care of some business obligations he agreed upon prior. He had many things going besides what he was doing with his family.

First, he had to go to the publishing house office in Manhattan. It was time for him to renew his book contract. The publishing house wanted to make him a new offer, which included a book contract extension.

Mike agrees to meet the publishing house representative on the next Monday morning. He made those plans on Tuesday.

That Wednesday evening when his flight arrived at JFK airport in queens. His wife was there to pick him up. She was happy to see him. She tells him that she missed him much. She gets out the car to give him a big hug and kiss.

He places his things inside the trunk of the car. He got into the car on the driver's side. His wife got on the passenger side. Then they drove off. In route, towards their destination, which was home.

Mike's wife tells Mike that Junior did very well on his term paper about his family history. Hearing that placed a smile on Mike's face. Also, while driving home, Mike spoke about everything that had taken place in the second meeting.

He mentions, the second meeting had a better turn-out than the first meeting did. His wife could not attend the second meeting because the kids had to go to school, and she had to work. So, keeping her up to speed. Letting her know what was going on, was the best solution.

Chapter 27
Pork Chop

On the way to the city Monday morning. Mike tells his driver to drop him off in his old neighborhood in Brooklyn. His driver questioned the move. Mike ensures his driver, that he will be all right.

He walked the same routes. He walked to the subway train station. Just like he did back in his college days. He reached the train station. He got a newspaper from the corner store, next to the subway.

Then he walked down the stair that led to the subway. He reached the subway platform. He looks around on the platform. He wanted to see who was on the platform with him.

He looks, into the subway tunnel in the direction the train will be coming from. He looks, but he sees no train lights inside the tunnel.

Since, no train was in sight. He decides to walk to the subway benches to sit down. He opens his newspaper and starts to read one of the articles inside.

He looks up from the wind of the express train provided when the train went through the train station.

He looks again to see who was on the platform. On the opposite side of the platform. He could not believe what he saw. He saw someone who looked like Pork Chop. A homeless elderly man talking to himself facing the wall.

Mike walks up the steps to get to the other platform. He walks down the stairs of the other platform. On the other side of the subway station. He walks up to who he thinks is Pork Chop.

Standing close but from a distance. He calls Pork Chop, Pork Chop. Pork Chop turns around. He looked at Mike. Pork Chop referred to Mike as the college kid.

Mike asked him, how was he doing? Pork Chop went on to say, hey college kid, you look older. Mike just laughed at what Pork Chop just said.

Then he asked Mike for a smoke. He wanted a cigarette. Mike politely told him that he does not smoke cigarettes. So, he did not have any to give.

Pork Chop tells Mike, he has not seen Chief in years. Mike breaks the bad news to him. He informs him that Chief had passed away. Pork Chop was clearly saddened by the news.

Little did Pork Chop know? That was not going to be the only news, he was going to get on that day.

Mike tells Pork Chop to pick up his belongings. He is going to take him somewhere. Pork Chop walked to his cardboard box. He began to collect his things. Mike thought about it.

He told Pork Chop, to leave all that stuff behind. Pork Chop agreed only if Mike bought him a pack of cigarettes. Mike agrees.

At first, Pork Chop was reluctant to go. To the point of he did not want to be bothered. After Mike persuaded him, more like bribed him. He explains to Pork Chop where he was taking him.

Pork Chop explains to him, the reason why him and Chief decided to live in the subway in cardboard boxes was because most of the men's homeless shelters were extremely dangerous for elderly men.

Honestly, he felt safer in the subway than the shelter system. Also, his main concern was a fresh new pack of cigarettes. Mike makes sure Pork Chop understood where he was taking him to, and he was going to be safe there.

It was, a haven for people, like him. Pork Chop liked what Mike was saying. But it seemed to be, too good to be true. He tells Mike, he better not be lying to him.

Because if he were, then not only would Mike have to buy him a pack of cigarettes, but he would also owe him a new cardboard box for him to live in.

They left the subway train station. The first place they stopped at was the corner bodega close to the train station. Where Mike purchased a pack of cigarettes for Pork Chop.

The store clerk did not want Pork Chop inside of the store. When Mike asked him why? He explains to Mike, he caught Pork Chop shoplifting.

Mike wanted to know what Pork Chop got caught shoplifting for. The store clerk laughs and says, he got caught shoplifting bread one day. He kept on laughing about it. Mike did not find any of it to be funny.

Mike knew the only reason why he tried to steal some bread was because obviously, he was hungry.

While Mike paid for the cigarettes, he also paid for the bread. He bought a cup of coffee and a sandwich for Pork Chop.

He understood the fact, Pork Chop was more than likely hungry now. He wanted to make sure Pork Chop got something to eat. When Mike gave the coffee and sandwich to Pork Chop.

Pork Chop looked to see what kind of sandwich it was. He saw it was a turkey sandwich. He asked Mike why didn't he buy him a ham sandwich? Mike smiles and chuckles about that.

Mike's goal was to take Norman Silverman, who was better known as Pork Chop, to live in a better place, that was safe and clean. Mike had the right place to take Norman to.

Mike calls his driver back to come pick him and Pork Chop up. Mike plans was to get Norman down south to the living center for adults, better yet the senior living center.

At that time, Mike did not care, either one of the living centers will fit fine. His main concern was to get Pork Chop down there.

Mike informs his driver to cover the seat with garbage bags. He lets his driver know, Pork Chop has not bathe in an exceedingly long time.

When his driver picked them up, his driver knew exactly what Mike was talking about. He drove with all the windows down. Mike's plan was to take Pork Chop to a cheap hotel room.

On the way, Mike stopped at a convenience store. Where he picked up some underwear and a tee-shirt. Sweatpants and cheap sneakers. Also, a lot of bathing products. Shaving cream and deodorant. And a disposable shaving razor. He purchases some socks and shampoo.

Then they headed to the hotel. He rented a room, he placed Norman inside. He instructs Pork Chop to take a shower and shave. Also, make sure he washes his hair.

Mike waited outside of the hotel room. Mike got on his cell phone to conduct the business he had planned to take care in Manhattan.

During this time, his driver took the car to the car wash. He wanted to get that smell out of the car as soon as possible.

After waiting for a nice while, Mike's driver came back with the car. That is when Mike decided to knock on the hotel room door. To check to see if Norman was all right.

After Pork Chop got dressed. When Pork Chop came out of the room.

At first, Mike thought he had the wrong room number. Because the wrong man opened the door. Until Pork Chop let him know, that it was him.

Mike and his driver were shocked about how clean Pork Chop looked. Very impressive to both. Mike took Norman to the barber shop. Pork Chop needed a haircut.

Then he took him clothes shopping, for some real clothes. That is when he learned what sizes Norman wore in clothes. He learned his sneaker and shoes sizes also.

With that knowledge Mike called his coordinator at the living center. He instructs her to prepare a room and get some clothes for Mr. Silverman. She took down all the information to get prepared for the arrival of Mr. Silverman.

He also wanted her to get in contact with his family if there were any? Before Mike turned in the hotel room key. He tells Norman to put on the new clothes he just purchased, for him.

Now, with the new clothes and shoes, with a haircut and a shower, he was ready to travel, looking nice.

Mike's driver knew Mike wanted him to drive them to the airport. Mike reserves plane tickets for the next available flight, from his phone app.

When they arrived at the airport. Mike calls his wife. He wanted to let her know what he was doing. She tells him, to be safe and she loved what he was doing.

When he told her that he found Pork Chop and they were waiting for their flight to take Pork Chop to the living center. She was blown away. She knew how much he wanted to find Pork Chop.

She remembers hearing about him when they were in college back in the day. This was one of the reasons why she fell in love with him. She admired his love for humanity.

The plane tickets costed him a pretty penny. Because it was last minute. He knew it was all worth it.

The men board their flight. The plane took off. On the plane Pork Chop mentions to Mike, the last time he was on a plane, was when he was coming home back from the Vietnam war.

He talked about how they went to the Vietnam war, as kids. He states, when they came back home as men back in the late 60's. Mostly all of them came home with alcohol and drug problems or both.

He did not go into details about that. Just like he did not talk about what led him to be in the current state he was in. Or why was he homeless in the first place.

Mike did not want to pressure him. That was not the reason why Mike was doing this for. They departed from the plane. Mike got a taxi to take them to their destination.

The coordinator got in touch with some of Norman's relatives. Which was his daughters. They did not live that far away. They were in route to the living center also.

They were looking forward to reuniting with their father. Who has been estranged from their family for so many years?

When the taxicab arrived in front of the living center. The first thing Pork Chop noticed was the name of the living center. He read the names of both buildings which was Chief Eagle living center for adults and Chief Eagle's senior living center.

That placed a smile on his face. He could not believe what he was seeing. He tells Mike, he must be dreaming. Mike reassures him, he was not dreaming at all.

Mike also mentions they were just getting started. Mike remembers when Chief told him the story. He remembers Pork Chop was there to witness it all.

So, Norman knew the significance of what he was seeing. Seeing it all, almost brought tears to Pork Chop's eyes. Mike walks into the center. He stops at the coordinator's office.

She gives him keys to the room Norman will be staying in. Mike opens the door to Norman's room, they walk in. Norman sees the size of the room he will be staying at. They walk around the huge room.

Mike goes and opens the closet door. He tells Pork Chop to come and check it out. The closet was full of new clothes. He looked down and saw a rack of sneakers and shoes.

He turns to Mike, to ask him whose clothes was this. He tells Mike, the clothes in the closet were some nice clothes.

He was ecstatic to find out, the clothes in the closet were his. He noticed the carton of cigarettes that was on the nightstand next to the bed. Mike informs him there was a designated area for smoking in the building.

Mike was also pleased with the choices his staff members came up with. The clothing selections they picked out was perfect for Mr. Silverman. Pork Chop asked Mike did he mind if he had a smoke. Mike reminds him to go to the smoking area in the building. Norman was happy and nervous all in one.

While Pork Chop was smoking his cigarette in the smoking area. His daughters arrived at the living center. They liked the way the outside of the building looked. They walked inside to where the receptionist was at. His daughters looked around, checking out the artwork on the walls of the waiting area.

They walked up to the front desk to inform the receptionist who they were. And who they came to see. The receptionist knew who they were, already. She was expecting them. She escorts them to the center's dayroom. After she gave them visitor's passes.

Norman's daughters brought their daughters along with them. Each one of Norman's daughters had daughters of their own. His oldest daughter had two sons and a daughter. His youngest daughter had two daughters and a son. Their sons were busy doing what they do. Their daughters were curious to see how their grandfather looked.

The receptionist told the group of women and girls that Mr. Silverman will be there shortly.

Just to top off this priceless moment. Norman was reunited with his family. That was the biggest surprise of the day for him.

When he saw his daughters. Is when tears came to and out of his eyes. Not only his, out of his daughters too. A touching moment. He did not see his daughters since they were little girls. And that was about 35 years ago.

Both parties were happy and excited to see one another. Mike came in the room to check to see if everything was okay. Mike walks up to the table where Norman and his daughters were sitting at. He introduces himself to the group of women and girls.

Then he placed a checkbook and a bank card on the table in front of Norman and his family. He informs Norman the checkbook and bank card was his. Mike was happy to let Norman know he has $100,000 in his bank account.

Norman's daughters were a little confused with Mike's gesture. Norman was too, he wanted to know what was the catch? His daughters did not know Mike. So, they wanted to question why was he being so generous to their father?

Norman tells his daughters he met Mike when Mike was in college. Pork Chop was beyond happy at that point. He felt like he had a fresh start of life. He thanked Mike for his kindness. His daughters and granddaughters thanked him too.

Mike told Pork Chop it was from his grandfather, who he did not know back then, Chief. Pork Chop had to paused for a moment. He had to let that sink in. He looks at Mike, he tells Mike he did notice that him and Chief was around the same height and body structure.

But he would have never guessed that. He smiled at Mike. He knew it was a connection. Because he knew firsthand, Chief did not open- up to just anybody.

Now, he knew what the connection was. Norman talked about how Chief used to always talk about him.

Mike wanted to do something special for his grandfather's best friend, neighbor, or whatever you want to call it. Norman tells Mike that he could still call him Pork Chop.

Pork Chop and Mike laughed about it. It was an inside joke. The only people who understood that was Pork Chop and Mike.

Mike left the dayroom. Norman stayed and got reacquainted with his daughters. They had a lot of catching up to do. His daughters started by introducing Norman to his three pretty granddaughters.

Chapter 28
Father's side

On the way back to New York. Mike felt just about completed. It was one more thing he needed to do, to make it all complete. Deep down inside, he knew what he had to address once and for all.

He spoke about it with his older brother. His brother told him, he reached out to him in jail. They wrote a couple of times. But after a while, there were no more contact. Mike reaches out to his mother. He wanted to know her opinion on this matter.

He wanted to know the whereabouts of his own father. For better or worse, he knew, he needed to find him. He felt it was the right thing to do.

Even though he did not appreciate nor liked the fact on how it all went down in his childhood. The way his father just upped and left them. To Mike it felt like his father left them in hell with nothing.

With one parent gone and the other one addicted to drugs, made it an extremely difficult. And a rough road for him and his siblings to grow up in those conditions.

Mike believes and understands time heals all wounds.

When he spoke to his youngest sister, she told him where their father was at. That was refreshing to know, because their mother did not have a clue where that man was at? And to be honest, the way she said it, she really did not want to know either.

Mike investigates into his father's history a little bit more. He wanted to find out more about the reason why his father was incarcerated? At the time his father was serving a 30-year prison sentence. He was in a prison upstate New York.

Mike goes and pays his father a visit. While he waited in the visiting area at a maximum prison upstate New York. He stares at the door where all the inmates were coming out of. The one is who had visitors.

He knew from looking up his father's case. He was aware of the fact; his father was a drug addict. His father was addicted to crack. Who murdered two people while robbing a gas station? He also knew his father served 29 years, out of a 30-year prison sentence.

To Mike's surprised, the prison guard rolled his father out. He was wheelchair bound.

His father had shackles on his feet connected to the wheelchair. Mike could not understand why would they do that? It is not like his father could get up and run away confined to a wheelchair. They had his father's hands handcuffed to the arms of the wheelchair.

He greets his father. His father sat there for a while. Trying to figure out who Mike was. Before he realized Mike was one of his sons?

But he still wasn't sure which one of his sons he was? Mike's father did not see his sons in so many years. It has been well over 3 decades since the last time Mike saw his father.

At first Mike's father thought he was his older brother. That is why he asked him, how long has he been home for? When did he get out of prison?

Mike told him, that was not him. He spares his father from thinking too hard. He lets him know he was his younger son.

Once Mike said that. His father knew exactly who he was. Mike asks his father, what was he going to do, once he gets released? His father did not have a clue about that.

To be honest, he always thought he was going to die in jail. He tells Mike, he never thought about it. Or took it into consideration, the question that Mike just asked him.

His father did not lie. He admits to the crimes, that he committed in the past. He talks about what had happened, by saying he was high on crack the day of the double homicide at the gas station robbery.

He acknowledges he deserved to be where he was at. He does apologize about not being there for his children. Also, not being there for the mother of his children.

He knew, he broke Mike's mother's heart in the process. The way he left was unacceptable, and he understood that. He did mention to Mike, he was a drug addict and a very violent person back then in his life.

He and Mike's mother had a very highly volatile and toxic relationship. On top of them both being addict to crack. With all of that turned into an unhealthy environment to raise children in.

He wanted Mike to understand, he was not making up any excuses. Merely, he was just stating the fact from his perspective.

A tear or two came out of his eyes, onto his wrinkled face. Mike's father stated his peace. Something he probably held bottled up for an exceptionally long time. That he needed to get off his chest. Mike felt the sincerity in the words his father spoke.

That is all he ever wanted was to hear his father's point of view about all of it. Mike asks his father, how he felt about leaving New York when he gets out of prison? Mike tells him about the living center for seniors.

Mike did not mention that he owns the place. Instead, he tells his father, he has a connection to get him in there. He thinks his father would be a perfect candidate to be placed there. His father did say that would be a good look.

Mike wanted to know a little more about his father's side of the family. His father tells him about his mother, Mike's grandmother. He tells him, his mother, was a schoolteacher, and an author of many books.

He also talks about Mike's grandfather being a jazz musician. Mike was interested and intrigued hearing about his grandparents. He wanted to hear more about them. He told his father that he was an English professor for a community college in the city.

He informed him that he too, was an author. At that moment they both knew where he got his writing gift from. The visit went great. They had a great conversation.

Mike left his father with a couple of books he authored. Mike left the prison feeling good. His father even told him, for all that is worth, he loves him.

Mike called his mother to tell her how it went. Mike's mother said something, he was not expecting her to say. She asked him, could his father be placed in the senior living center?

Mike needed to know, where she got her idea from? He knew his mother did not come up with that one. She told him, his sister asked her about it. His mother lets him know that she said yes to the idea.

She said, she talked to the coordinator at the senior living center already. She tells Mike the paperwork was being processed. All they were doing was waiting on his father's release date.

Mike felt like they must have read his mind. He felt good, he did not have to ask.

Unfortunately, Mike's father passed away in prison, the day before his release date. Mike's point was made. He made peace with his father. At that time, and moment. That is what made Mike, feel completed.

Chapter 29
Woman Chief

After the passing of Mike's grandmother. His mother decided to leave New York City for good. At first, she was just using her house down south as a summer getaway for her and her mother.

Now, she wanted to be down there for good. Mike's mother found peace and quiet living on the same land her father, her father's father, and so forth, lived on. She takes many strolls to the river in her back yard, that was connected to the land.

She created a huge garden of fruits and vegetables. She donates her fruits and vegetables to the town's food bank for the homeless people. And the people in the shelter.

Next to that, she created a huge garden of flowers. Every day she takes flowers to the tribe's burial site. Which was located a little further down on the property near the river.

Mike calls his mother just about every day, to see how she was doing? She thanked him for all he has done for their family. She told him, he was the rock that kept it all together, through it all. She went on to tell him, she was blessed to have a son like him.

Mike was the type of person, who helps everyone. Sadly enough, not too many acknowledged the fact, to at least say thank you, sometimes. Not saying he does what he does for any of that. It is simply good to hear it, sometimes.

After having a wonderful, heartfelt, conversation with his dearly beloved mother. A couple of days later. His mother passes away.

With the passing of his mother. All she had was divided in 4 ways. Representing her four children. Mike, his brother and his 2 sisters. All, of her children agreed to bury their mother on the property.

During the construction of the living centers, the construction men discovered a burial site. An old graveyard. His brother called him about it. Mike told them not to touch that.

In fact, he instructs them to put a fence around the whole grave site. And that is how the tribal burial site was put back, where it belongs, in the hands of the people of the tribe.

When his mother passed away, she was buried there. At the ancestral tribe's burial site. Along with all the other natives of the land, her ancestors.

The aboriginals of this land. Her children bought her a huge tombstone to honor her name and legacy. The first female Chief Eagle of the tribe.

Chapter 30
Identity

Through it all, they never lost respect for their mother. No matter what had happened or what she has been through. They all were proud to be called her children.

Mike wanted to know some more about his father's side of the family. After his father told him about his grandmother was an author too.

Mike had to find out more about that. He went online to a vintage bookstore website. To look it up. Mike knew all books had ISBN numbers. Which is recorded. And any book can be found under these numbers.

He typed in her name. He wanted to see if anything pops up. Just like his father had told him. A bunch of book titles his grandmother wrote flooded his computer screen.

He plans on reading all those books his grandmother wrote. Seeing all of them books caught his curiosity? He began reading a book his grandmother wrote entitled, Tribal Nations. This book was about different tribes.

The aboriginals of the land before European discovery. And how many of the tribes got reclassified as colored. Or, even African.

Mike realized his family on his father's side was tribal people too. When he told his older brother about what he discovered.

All they could do was look at each other and shake their heads in disbelief over how much they have been lied to about this in their lives. Finally, they obtained the truth.

His brother told Mike about an idea, he had. He asked Mike, would he be interested in partnering up with him. Going half on a property on the other side of the road from the living centers.

Mike's brother explains to Mike about an abandoned property. He just found out about. That was up for sale from the town. Mike wanted to see more about what his brother was talking about. His brother did one better. He drove Mike to the land. So, he could get a look at the land first-hand.

Mike and His brother got out of his brother's car. They stood on the abandoned land. The first thing, Mike saw on the land, was a big, abandoned house that was ran down.

Then he looks in the other direction, he saw a huge field where many crops could be planted. It was difficult to see what grew in the field.

Because of the upkeep of the property. It looked like nobody touched this land in over a hundred years or more?

Clearly, he began to put all the pieces together. Everything was exactly the way Chief explained it, when he was telling Mike the story, back then.

Mike and his brother were amazed on how accurate the story was. His brother picks up a hat. That looked like a crown. That was made, out of feathers.

With out any words being said. They knew what the Chief's hat meant. And what it stood for.

After seeing undeniable evidence of what this land was. Mike's brother takes out his phone, to see who was the previous owner of the property?

When he saw the name Andrew Parker. He showed the name to Mike. Mike saw Andrew Parker. That was all the confirmation they needed.

Mike agrees to go half with his brother. They agreed before they tear anything down and begin to build on the land.

First, they wanted to study, show, tell and teach their family the significance of this discovery.

How the book and this place went hand and hand, with their heritage. There was so much to learn on this land. Mike hires an archaeologist to do an excavation on the land site.

The archaeologist discovered so much evidence of the people who were on the land for thousand of years. He found different tools and bones that went back thousands of years.

Mike's plan was for the archaeologist to collect all the things he discovers. During the excavation Mike invites his family to get an up-close and personal look and experience of their family's history, on the land their family roamed for centuries.

The first one to come visit the land was Mike's youngest son, Mark. Mark was now the mayor of the city where the town was located in. Mark came to tears. He knew this was his family's history.

Also, he knew his father's compassion about finding out their family history. He knew that since he was a little boy. He knew what it all meant to his father.

By this time Mike's family provided so many jobs for the residents of the town. Not only at the living centers. Mike's sisters came from out of town. They told him, they had to see this for themselves.

When Mike, his brother and sisters stood on the land of master's Parker which he stole from their ancestors in the first place.

To have all their land back in their family's possession. A place, once upon a time that was where their tribe lived in peace in harmony, for thousands of years.

Mike and his siblings stood together on their family's land. It was an emotional moment for everyone in the family. Words could not hardly describe the feeling. But the moment was priceless.

Mike wanted to make a museum of his family's aboriginal presence on this land. A documented history of the tribe. That will teach the family's history.

Not only just for his family's generations to come. But also, to anyone who wants to learn about his culture and history.

He wanted it, to be made for the public. Like any other public museum. Many years have passed. Since him and his family opened the senior living center. It was many decades ago when he first met Chief and Pork Chop.

While they celebrated the 20-year anniversary of the living centers. Mike was now a senior citizen himself. You could almost say he lives at the living center. Since he was there all the time.

Especially, after the passing of his beloved wife. Through the years his brother and his sisters all passed away. Mike was practically alone at this point. His children were adults themselves with their own families and their own lives to live. Mike hung out with Pork Chop most of the time.

Even though Pork Chop was in his late 80's at this point. And Mike had a nurse's aide push Pork Chop in his wheelchair around. Sitting watching television game shows was how they spent most of their days.

During one of them commercials, after seeing the one about ancestry. Norman wanted to try it out. So, they did what he wanted. The results came back. It displayed his family tree. It when back a couple of generations.

Pork Chop asked Mike, who he still called College kid, to read the results.

Mike places his reading glasses on his face. He begins to read it out loud. Mike starts from the top of the page. He discovers that Pork Chop was not lying after all. He reads that Pork Chop's great grandmother name was Lilly.

Mike thought nothing of it. So, he kept on reading the chart for Pork Chop. Pork Chop insisted that Mike read what he just read again. He wanted to make sure he heard, what he just heard.

Mike read that a woman named Lilly was an Indian and she was his great grandmother. She had Pork Chop's father in a small town in Illinois. Not too far away from Chicago.

Still Mike did not catch on. About a year later Pork Chop passes away. Mike mainly stayed to himself after that. His oldest grandson who started college in the city, the town, where the living centers were in.

He comes to visit His grandfather Mike when he gets a chance. He rolls his grandfather to his favorite spot. Which was by the lake. That day Mike told his grandson a story about a tribe who lived peacefully on their land.

While he was telling his grandson the story. When he got to the part about his great, great, Grandmother April. And how she had a sister named Lilly. Who was half Indian and half white? Who could pass for white? Due to the fact of Master Parker impregnated one of his slaves.

Then it hit Mike. That is when he realized that Chief and Pork Chop were distant cousins. Their grandmothers were sisters. Mike paused for a moment.

He sat in silence until his grandson asked him, was he all right. Mike said yes. Then he got back to the story he was telling his grandson who was in college.

Everything came into fruition with Mike finding out about that. Mike's soul was completely settled. This was a story that kept on giving. That is what Mike learned about it.

Also, it became a story that repeats itself. From generation to generation. This family history will never die. The ancestors made sure of that. Their family history story will be passed down.

And Mike was the one who finally documented it. He put it on paper. His tribe got their land taken away, because of documentations. And he got their land back with documentations.

Mike was able to rest in Peace with a smile on his face.